€$CAP€?

by

NIK KRASNO

**Hosting a guest – star: Graeme Rodaughan,
the author of Metaframe War series**

NEPLOKHO PUBLISHING

ISBN 978-0-9930827-4-0

If you are Quentin Tarantino, Guy Ritchie or an aspiring director interested in adapting this book into a movie, please, feel free to contact the author.

This is a work of fiction. Names, characters, businesses, organizations, countries, places, events and incidents either are the product of the author's imagination or are used

Preamble

Sometime 2020 (before or after the outbreak of the Coronavirus), Somewhere

I hated waking up tied in the trunk of a speeding car. Never did it before, but the second I came to my senses I knew it. I tried to move my hands, but they were handcuffed. Eyes covered with blinds, a gag in my mouth.

I was left with a sense of smell, and the stench of machine oil was unbearable. *What the fuck did they keep here before my precious self?*

The next thought was *Great, Misha, what have you gotten yourself into?* Exasperated, cynical, disoriented, soon to become panicky – I was all of these at once, conducting a dialog with myself, feeling numbness in most of my limbs and fast-developing respiratory problems.

The staccato of a machine gun made me stop fidgeting and trying to find a little room.

Damn, they are shooting at us! A bullet hissed near the trunk, another one hit the car somewhere. The car started to "dance" on the road, zigzagging.

Chasing or being chased, I didn't like either set-up. I was simultaneously trying to reconstruct in my mind the preceding chain of events.

The car jumped, and my forehead crashed into the lid. For a second there I felt knocked out.

A machine gun went into action again. This time it sounded closer.

Another round. I felt an acute pain in my left leg, and a second later another bullet hit my arm, passing through it into my chest. *I'm hit,* I thought, before passing out.

Chapter 1
Incarcerated

My eyes were closed, yet light nonetheless penetrated into my brain. The eyelids couldn't stop its prying strength. The sense of *déjà vu* told me I was in a coma again. *Misha, wake up, open your eyes!* I didn't want the coma. Different thoughts raced about my mind, but one thing I knew: *I wouldn't give up trying.*

The second attempt was more successful. I managed to open my right eye. The left one hurt and wouldn't open.

Seeing the annoying spot lamp directed straight at my face and an empty room, its lower half painted dirty blue and the upper half dirty white, ejected me into reality, which I wanted to escape so much. It was just a recurrent dream, which kept haunting me when I fainted.

I was tied to the chair, beaten, and left alone for a while, probably soon to be tortured again.

In rare moments of bitter sarcasm, I called this an "escape room," referring to such places where I'd been with my kids. How easy it was there – find one clue after another, sometimes with the generous help of a guide, and no matter what – in forty minutes you were out. In my case, I felt I was stuck in the room for weeks, although I lost track of time and couldn't know for sure, and escape was an unattainable dream. Damn, I'd rather choose a coma again!

I heard voices in the corridor. Approaching.

A second later, a pair of everyday torturers entered the room. Judging by their sadistic smiles, they were in an excellent fucking mood. Something I hadn't experienced for a long time.

"Misha, every time I enter the room, I'm dignified with hosting the richest man on the planet in my modest quarters. Don't the superrich deserve to suffer sometimes too? I've got the results of your medical examinations." Senya (that's what he was called by his partner) was beaming. "Some of your injuries may become irreversible, my friend. The orthopedist here mentions that you might not be able to walk anymore and, knowing your promiscuity, the urologist suspects developing problems with erections." The cunt laughed out loud, evidently pleased with himself.

The other guy, Gennady, never showed much emotion and remained indifferent. These two were sadists. They proved it to me many times over. Unfortunately, their instrument of proof was me. Gennady did the dirty part – breaking me - while Senya never touched me, probably from hygienic concerns, but his wry grin betrayed that he was enjoying watching every punch and torture Gennady applied.

I was too dizzy to fully comprehend what Senya was saying. He, on the other hand, knew it would sink in sooner rather than later.

They wanted my money. All of it and more, even the imaginary sums I had never had and, of course, they didn't want me alive after that.

"The bullet in your brain will look like a kids' game in comparison with what we'll inflict on you here, Misha. You may consider yourself a hero, but I doubt anyone will ever applaud your resistance. Why do you need so much money anyway?"

We returned to our usual dialogue: they wanted the money, in amounts I didn't have and which I just couldn't deliver. Those journals offering arbitrary wealth valuations can lead to a big disservice!

"Listen, I told you one hundred times and I repeat it again: I don't have that much dough. True, I probably could've taken it, but I made the Magnificent Seven spend it instead. On philanthropy. None of it went to me. Until I met you, I thought I had enough of my own. Obviously, you don't believe me, as you keep demanding a trillion dollars from me. I'm a billionaire, now a captive one, not a trillionaire. Don't you think I'd save my fucking life, if I could?" I was frustrated because there was no chance I could comply with their demands, nor convince them. It was beyond all their known canons that someone could simply blow that much moolah, when having a chance to take it all for himself.

And they were right from their perspective. For any noble move on my part, I always had a terrible backfire, as if doing something good was against my nature. Too frequently my selfless acts were frustrated and beaten, this time literally. Everyone, including my best friend David, thought I was nuts surrendering astronomic amounts from the Magnificent Seven for some ephemeral "greater good." Did I regret it, making the Seven spend it? Admittedly, when tortured – yes, but at the back of my mind I still thought I'd done something valuable.

However, my captors were the least likely crowd to appreciate it. Altruism, selflessness existed somewhere, but not very distinct and more for disguise, especially in this part of the globe. All my intuition told me I was kept in Russia. Where else can you find this ugly decoration for a room, primitive shaky wooden chair and worn out army mattress? For too long I grew up among these things, so I recognized them right away. Senya's accent and manners, though, betrayed someone who spent most of his life speaking English for a mother tongue.

"Why do you need this kind of money anyway?" Speaking meant not being beaten, so I preferred to converse.

"None of your business, but I don't mind telling you. To change the world, of course."

I couldn't discern whether he was solemn or sarcastic.

Meanwhile, Senya's good mood evaporated and his sinister self came forth.

"You, fucker, give up on yourself. It'll be interesting to see what you'll do when your son is sitting beside you."

I really feared this eventuality, however hoped that after my abduction the remaining members of my security protocol would guard my family tightly - so tightly that these bastards wouldn't have access to any of my relatives.

"Senya, I offered you fifty billion bucks. That's pretty much what I have, save for small change. Take it, leave me alone. I've done what I've done and pose no threat to anyone. You can split it with whoever's behind you. That's much more

9

than any of you would ever be able to steal or make. Be humble and reasonable, because if I die, which can also happen, according to the medical examinations you've mentioned, this money will be gone."

I sensed greed in him and more of it among those whom he represented. I was their prize chicken to produce a golden egg. And still they didn't believe me and interpreted my willingness to part with all my capital as a sign of my having more - a trillion extorted from the Seven.

It was a stalemate: they couldn't kill me (yet); I couldn't provide what they wanted. Just when I thought I had enough to afford anything I wanted I couldn't even buy my freedom.

Battered and dejected, but still able to think through surging pains of my broken limbs, I knew I needed to escape - but I couldn't do it by myself. Help could come only from the outside.

Chapter 2
London, Mikhail Vorotavich's headquarters
<u>Sober consultation</u>

Sasha couldn't say he wasn't prepared. Misha, his younger brother, was always in some kind of jam. Trouble was his fate and also a source of his now epical wealth. But everything has a toll. Once, the main hall of Misha's mansion was full of friends and associates; now, in this critical moment, it hosted only Sasha and David, Misha's best friend.

Both felt orphaned, with Arthur – their chief of security – slaughtered, and Misha – the mastermind – apparently abducted.

All "hot pursuit" options were exhausted, emergency calls made and initial shock settled. Nothing helped. They were confronted with the cold reality that they didn't have the slightest clue as to Misha's whereabouts, whether he was dead or alive, nor what his captors were after. It so happened that Misha had half the world (more literally than virtually) among his enemies. Powerful men from political echelons and business communities in numerous countries would gladly have him captive or -- better – dead.

"Dave, we need to identify this 'Suzy' bitch and proceed from there, since she's the only lead we have." Sasha stated the obvious, referring to Suzy's disappearance concomitantly with Misha's after killing Arthur and injecting something into Misha. The security cameras recorded some of the tragic events that preceded the kidnapping. Likely not acting alone, Suzy was the executor if not the main figure. Was she really "Suzy" or was it just her fake identity? They were groping in the dark. After leaving the mansion, Suzy -- and Misha with her -- evaporated, leaving no further trace anywhere. Airports, border control, street cameras, and intelligence reports contained no further clue.

"Yeah, it's unbelievable how Arthur with all his experience didn't even think she was all false – from identity to intentions. Love is blinding even for weathered veterans." Dave shared his regret. This was their first strategic discussion after the mess of hectic, disorganized efforts exhausted itself without helping much.

"Might take time, but we have her fingerprints, as well as photos. With unlimited resources at our disposal, we should be able to find some trace. Yeah, she'd likely changed her appearance, so placing her portrait everywhere might not help much."

"Agree," David nodded. "Let's analyze what we know again. She worked for Richard Avenue and that's where Misha got her from. Unfortunately, Richard is dead; however, we can try to trace her through his associates. This should be handled by…"

"Wait!" Sasha interrupted. "We need to check all foreign female visitors entering Ukraine a few days before Boris's funeral. Remember, she passed Misha a note at the cemetery. There shouldn't be that many."

"Right, good idea!" Dave cheered. "Couldn't be too many. I'll contact the border control chief. Can only hope she entered under her true identity."

"We must do everything we can. Maybe we'll find a false Suzy again, but at least we will have tried. What were you saying before I interrupted you?"

The wrinkles on Dave's face become deeper. "Right... Oh, I wanted to suggest Kevin to head the 'Richard' branch of the investigation. He's former Scotland Yard and energetic enough to make a few hops around the globe, if necessary, and return with quick answers."

Sasha didn't know him much, so he just shrugged. "Let him. Investigating will take time, but we need to get to the bottom of who she is, as she's our only link to what happened."

David put out his cigarette, admitting to himself that he'd been smoking too much since Misha disappeared. He took his mobile phone out of his jacket's inner pocket, typed the name on the contact list and dialed Mr. Polyvoda - the commissioner of the border police of Ukraine.

Locating someone who could be anywhere on the planet under an unknown identity wasn't an easy task. Maybe Suzy wasn't as capable in hiding as Bin Laden, but how to find someone trained to disappear, especially when she knew they'd be looking?

Chapter 3
Tortured

This is the end... The Doors' hit was constantly playing in my head. Unsurprisingly. After what had become a routine round of beatings, I was untied and left alone.

I hoped the fuckers wouldn't return during the rest of the day. A tiny square of light behind the bars went dimmer, signaling the approach of the evening.

I crawled towards the mattress, as I couldn't walk; Gennady had broken my right ankle, and my left one was still healing from a bullet wound. I hoped I would have a chance to even the score with the brute one day. Not something realistic in the given situ.

This is the end... I needed to change my mood to try to analyze whether there might be something I hadn't thought about. And I thought a lot. Even about weird stuff, like offering my captors to buy shares of corporations under my control only to sell them at the spike caused by the news of my release. They didn't buy my idea.

This time they had left an assortment of newspaper parts for me, carefully selected to portray my disappearance.

Through pain, I couldn't resist my curiosity -- not that I had anything else to do. I didn't know exactly how many days had passed, but I still couldn't get used to doing nothing.

Restless, suffering from pains all over my body, especially the broken right leg, I leafed through the different angles provided by the media.

The *English Times* gave little attention to my abduction, apart from the bombastic heading "The Richest Man Disappears," which was replicated in various forms everywhere. It didn't cast much light, giving the date when I was reported missing and stating that for a long time I had been rumored to have ties with the Russian – Ukrainian mafia and that this could explain my abrupt disappearance from the radar. They chose to place an explicitly ugly photo of me. *Wait for a suit, bastards!* I had a bliss to forget where I was for a sec.

My own memories and comprehension of the abduction were patchy. I saw Arthur down on the floor with a cut throat, surrounded by a pond of blood, and Suzy injecting me with something before I passed out. I had come to my senses inside a car trunk, blindfolded and gagged, unable to grasp much. Then – blackness until I reappeared in this room. I vaguely remembered someone making another injection in between.

A German business newspaper apparently provided bigger coverage with a nice picture of me and David. I couldn't read German; however, scrutinizing the article, I spotted here also the word "mafia" two or three times.

Russian newspapers had more recent dates than the others, which corroborated my suspicion that I was being held in Russia. Most of them emphasized my confrontation with the Western business community and authorities, mentioning only briefly my "problems" with the Russian Federation. Allowing for censorship, I assumed they didn't want to draw suspicions.

I unscrewed the top of the plastic water bottle and took a big gulp.

Finally, the *Boston Guardian* gave a somewhat broader account of search attempts, mentioning the formal complaint about my disappearance and futile attempts of the authorities and private investigators to uncover any details. My crying wife's photo was there with a caption reading, "Family in despair."

Crude work, fuckers. As the articles were deliberately selected, I knew my captors wanted to stress how emptyhanded were the rescue attempts, if any.

Arthur's death must've resonated in the press too, and I was sure my abduction should've been linked to it, but none of these were among the articles I was given.

Even without the reports, I knew that my associates would have much trouble finding me in Russia, not to mention extracting me from here. Being a fervent supporter of Ukraine in its conflict with a heavyweight neighbor, I knew that influential Russians would shun contacting me. Thus, my connections in Russia were weaker than elsewhere. Arthur had been a former Russian commando who had his moves, so having him out of the game rendered the chances even slimmer.

This is the end, beautiful friend...

Chapter 4
Welcome to Canada

Kevin, a cynic like almost everyone with long and eventful life experience of "been there, done that," nonetheless was a pro.

Looking strong and younger than his actual age of 45, he resembled a retired sportsman rather than a spook. Not that he was enthused with his new assignment -- excitement was just not his nature -- but he approached the matter with the required diligence. He had studied all open source info about the late Richard Avenue, including his family and business associates; he had ordered what he could from MI5 databases using personal connections; he had asked Sergey, Arthur's deputy, for info from Russian secret databases and had scheduled and mapped out those he'd chosen to interview.

Procuring info from closed sources would cost, but he worked for the richest dude on the planet, so a few grand wasn't even an issue.

They all knew Suzy had been Richard's confidante. For obvious reasons, Kevin thought Richard might not as eagerly share Suzy's status with his wife and family in general, so he put Richard's biz circle at the priority. If he were introduced, he could maybe skip some personal meetings, but he needed a recommendation from one of

Avenue's employees. He scheduled the first in-person meeting with Mrs. Dooling, Richard's ex-head of HR.

He boarded a plane after making sure the aircraft wasn't one of the new Boeings crashing recently, and the trip to Toronto was uneventful. His neighbor in first class was sucked into his laptop even before take-off. Trying to arrive fresh, Kevin slept most of the trip.

So far, so good. The change came quickly.

Kevin took a cab to reach the hotel, having a few good hours before meeting Mrs. Dooling. Immersed in his thoughts, rehearsing the questions he intended to ask, Kevin didn't pay much attention to the surroundings. He'd been to Toronto once a while back, but this time he wasn't into sightseeing.

"Thirty-five dollars." The driver turned around and stared at Kevin.

Baffled by seeing nothing but countryside, Kevin was automatically reaching for his wallet when a spray of gas hit his face. Before he was even able to understand what was happening, a heavy blow to his face made him scream. And then another and another one. Bombarded with punches, Kevin tried to cover his face with both arms, hoping the tear gas effect would weaken. *I wish I'd brought weapons!*

A momentary pause in beating allowed the driver to step out, open the back door, and try to pull Kevin out. Fearing for his life, Kevin pressed both hands hard against the car's walls, opposing hysterically the attempt to get him out.

All of a sudden, a kick from behind hurled him out of the car like a champagne cork from a bottle. *Where did another one appear from?*

Two pairs of legs continued the kicking job. He closed his eyes, coiled, and covered his head with both arms.

"You faggot, return to London!" "Go for the face!" "You never come here again!" His assailants were heating each other up.

"Look at this one." Kevin felt full well a boot hitting an unprotected part of his skull.

"Enough," said one of them -- according to the voice, probably the driver.

Kevin felt himself being frisked.

"You leave Canada and cease your attempt to go after Avenue, Vorotavich, anyone. If you or your bosses persist, next time we won't spare you."

The car sped away, leaving Kevin blinded and lying by the gutter.

What the fuck was that? Kevin expected anything, but not being beaten even before getting to meet the lady.

After the tear gas effect dwindled, he looked around trying to understand where he was and to find his belongings on the ground. His passport and wallet were there. The cellphone was, too, but busted by a blow of something sharp against its front glass.

Kevin made a quick damage control check-up: bleeding and bruised, but otherwise intact. His left leg hurt and that wasn't helpful, as he couldn't see anything but endless road ahead. His heeled inspector shoes, posh business suit, and just a light jacket were the worst possible outfit for a long hike.

He squinted. The road seemed deserted.

Slowly the rage started to prevail over all other emotions. *What an ambush!* he thought angrily. These guys were too knowledgeable about his business here in Canada.

And primarily he was angry with himself. So engaged with his upcoming meeting, he was trapped and fooled like a rookie! *Alright, now it's personal.* The shame of posing little opposition to the assailants was another strong feeling that wouldn't relent. The only time he had been so severely and one-sidedly beaten was by football hooligans back in high school.

A low-flying plane, obviously on a descent, meant that they hadn't gotten too far from the airport. The wilderness around him seemed improper; he was supposed to be near a big city, after all.

Lamenting didn't help and the chilly gusts prompted action. Although the landing route of the airplane indicated the direction of the airport further down the road, Kevin chose the direction he had come from. He started walking, hoping to catch a ride at some point, while considering this unexpected development.

There was a leak somewhere. Unlikely from the woman he had scheduled to meet. Somebody had intercepted his communication with Mrs. Dooling. Either their office in London was compromised or Avenue's headquarters. Both were equally likely. Kevin was further annoyed with himself for taking no precautions and planning no counter-measures.

Normally, he'd report at the first opportunity what had happened to Arthur, but with Arthur's being dead, Kevin was hesitant whether he wanted to look like a silly boy in front of David and others. The position of VP security was open and, if Kevin aspired to take it, such a blunder on his part would blow all his chances.

No, it's between me and them. I've been beaten, no need to humiliate myself any further.

After an hour and a half, when Kevin was desperately thinking that he'd need to walk all the way, a car appeared on the road behind him.

No time for pleasantries – he just stood in the middle of the road, waving his hands, hoping the driver would elect not to run him over. It was a close call, as the car stopped just a few centimeters from him.

The driver opened the window, probably holding his foot tight on the gas pedal.

"What is it?"

"Sorry, Sir, for interrupting your journey. I came from abroad and a taxi driver mugged me and left me here. I'd appreciate a ride to any place with public transportation. I've got money. I can pay!" Kevin tried to sound polite.

"If you were mugged, how is it that you have money?" The driver was still suspicious.

Damn, he's right!

"I have a hidden pocket they didn't find. The cab man just took my wallet." Kevin enhanced his London accent to sound touristic. He did have two grand stashed separately as company's cash, allocated for the business trip.

"Get in. I see the mugger roughed you up. You need some help."

The driver was a nice guy after all. He dropped Kevin off in Toronto, making sure he had a taxi to take him further to the hotel.

So far, Canada had turned out not exactly hospitable. Kevin didn't know it yet, but more surprises lay ahead.

Chapter 5
Opportunity

These guys were amateurs. Wicked, brutal, arrogant, but amateurs. My confidence in that conclusion grew every day. It was the small things: the compound they held me in and lax procedures - sometimes they'd search the room meticulously and make sure nothing was there, other times they'd just leave me spoons for the whole day; their faulting references to different businessmen as their sponsors (I knew some of them and I still had a good memory) and since they belonged to rival clans proved they were bullshitting; their lack of knowledge of basic financial terms and how childishly they imagined my wealth; the way they interrogated me; this mysterious Paul they'd referenced as their guru – surely if he was someone worth knowing, I would have heard his name; as well as bizarre organizations they supposedly represented.

Not that this knowledge helped in any way, but I thought relentlessly about how I could use their ineptitude to my benefit. My days were numbered. I knew my body and, unless I got out, they'd torture me to death or my injuries would deteriorate. They took me to the shower a few times, but I still felt like I was rotting together with the rotten mattress and everything around me. Convincing them to take what I could procure – that just wasn't enough for their appetite. Indeed, why bargain if they believed my actual wealth to be as reported on maybe twenty internet sites -- estimates skewed to a much greater than real number. I wished this Paul were here, for I thought I'd have better chances to convince someone smarter and more reasonable than these clowns, but his visit wasn't in the cards.

Just thinking couldn't help, of course, so I acted. Aluminum wasn't hard to break. Bending and unbending the spoon they'd left in the room, I managed to detach the handle. It was sharp, but maybe not rigid enough. I hid it in the mattress. It was full of holes anyway and they didn't check every single one.

Today I repeated the trick with another spoon. Having two spoon handles made me "armed and very dangerous." *Yeah, right.*

Of course, I tried to pick the lock on the door during the night. It wasn't locked with the inbuilt lock, but apparently with a hanging lock on the outside. *Shit.*

Sneaking out wasn't an option. Yeah, I had read *The Count of Monte Cristo* and imagined digging a hole or a tunnel or just around the metal bars on the windows, but that would take years, which I didn't have. Dumas's recipe wasn't for those undergoing daily tortures.

Given no other choice, I needed to confront my opponents. It was a suicidal idea, but at this point it didn't matter. Being on death row meant I had no alternatives.

I didn't know what awaited me behind the door where I was locked, so I could make only approximate planning, but that was stage two. Stage one was getting through this fucking white, shabby metal door.

The opportunity presented itself soon. No voices, just the steps. Somebody was approaching. I lay on the floor on my back, arms open, with a "weapon" hidden in each torn sleeve of what was once a sweater.

It must've looked grotesque – me feigning dead or unconscious. I lay there motionless with my heartbeat on two hundred, pounding in my ears from anxiety.

I didn't dare keep my eyelids even slightly open. Who came in didn't matter. Whoever it was, he rushed to me and pressed his ear to my chest to check what was up. Just what I expected. I stabbed the fucker in his throat with my right arm and then again and again. He screamed, blood gushing all over, tried to get up and move away from me, but I held him tight with my left hand, stabbing him again and again, anywhere I could reach. It was Gennady -- I saw him at this point – and he deserved every blow and more.

Finally, he quieted. I knew I had just seconds before someone came to check out all the shrieks and noise.

Trembling from what I'd done, I went for his gun, which he kept under his shirt. Seeing the door opening, I released the safety and rolled sideways to get a better angle at it.

In order to see this part of the room, he needed to enter or put his head out from behind the door. The stupid fucker entered and I "greeted" him with two shots. The body dropped, swinging the door wide open. Some guard I hadn't seen before.

Now I had to move. I crawled, as I couldn't stand on my legs. I peeped out of the room: a corridor -- empty, but long. *Fuck!*

I crawled forward, adrenaline fueling me like a healing elixir. My personal body count grew and with it my animality.

Suddenly, I saw a shadow. I stopped and took aim. A new opponent didn't jump into my sight headlong.

I frequented the shooting gallery that Arthur had built in the basement of my mansion, and I wasn't his worst disciple. Maybe not a sniper, but to aim and shoot I knew. *How many bullets does a TT have?!* I recognized the gun, but couldn't remember its capacity.

As soon as I saw his head moving from behind the corner I went for the shot and added two more just to the corner of the wall, hoping bullets would pierce through. Somebody yelped. I'd wounded another one! I crawled further when the gun appeared where the head was and started shooting randomly.

I tried to glue myself to the wall, waiting until the barrel stopped throwing death. Luckily all his shots missed, while I tried to be as flat as a wall painting.

Steadying my arm and aiming as carefully as I could, I shot at the hand holding the gun. I hit the gun, and the hand holding it dropped it. It was in my sight. I moved further, ready to shoot if its owner tried to grab it.

I heard him running down the stairs, retreating. *Wise move, fucker.*

I was sure he'd be calling for reinforcements in a few moments. Every second counted.

Already sensing freedom, I nonetheless stopped. I needed a car! And for it - the keys. Almost every action movie had this episode with starting the engine by connecting two wires, but I didn't think I could repeat the trick.

Just when time was so precious, and against all my yearning prompting me to get out, I crawled back to the room and frisked Gennady and the second guy I had shot.

Both had rings with keys on them. The wallets and cell phones would do, too. I took them with me. And another gun. When you want to live, crawling is not a problem.

Now, I was well armed and dangerous. This time for real.

Determined to get out, I moved to my freedom. It was a pathetic flight, but I was still on my way out!

The engine noise of the approaching cars immediately killed my enthusiasm.

Chapter 6
Apprehended

Misha's disappearance was a real crisis overlaying David's invented middle life crisis. In his forties, he had become less agile and more reflective. Still full of black and caustic humor in public, when alone he was much less joyful.

Misha and he had made it big time. No doubt. But was it worth losing Boris and Arthur on the way and Johnny, his wife's brother, although spared but expelled by Misha never- to- be- seen anywhere around? And where was Misha now? Although Michael showed the ability for resurrection like the mythological phoenix, David's skepticism of his ability to pull it off again grew with every day that passed. Maybe Misha's fortunes could save his ass, but if that was the case, he would have expected his kidnappers to press some demands by now. Finally, David himself had barely survived on more than one occasion.

He hoped their story wasn't finished yet. Eccentric introvert as Misha was, very few knew him really well and even fewer understood him. When Michael had forced the Magnificent Seven to part with their wealth and hadn't taken a penny for himself, David was only half surprised. Some thought of Misha as an overgrown, infantile, and reckless adventurer or a cynical and shrewd business shark/mafia boss or a lucky and ballsy opportunist, crazy about women. But those who got to know him closer discovered a big heart and lots of good intent.

Kevin's call caught him in the midst of these deliberations.

"Hi, Kevin, how is it going?"

"Much worse than we thought." Kevin described what had happened.

Playing it calm as much as he could, David still felt shock and anxiety emanating from Kevin. "Holy shit. Where did they know from?" David's abstract thoughts rerouted to a practical course immediately.

"That's the interesting part. I doubt it could have come from Avenue's people's direction, for I didn't tell them the details of my arrival, flight and all. It's from us. We either have a mole or they tracked our London office or hacked into our system somehow. I'm inclined to believe the latter version. Would be good if our cyber people checked it out."

This was unexpected. David didn't anticipate an active countering of their attempts to locate Michael.

"Sure, Kevin. I'm on it. Keep yourself safe. If necessary, hire bodyguards to accompany you while there. These dudes hardly expect us to heed their threats. Once they are sure we are proceeding, they will escalate their opposition."

"Yeah, at least I take it that we are looking in the right direction, if they don't want me in Canada that much. Let me call Mrs. Dooling to reschedule the meeting. I'll call back later."

***

Kevin's next call remained unanswered, as were the subsequent ones. He spent half a day calling and emailing Mrs. Dooling. What the hell had happened? Yes, he had missed the meeting, but she couldn't know it was him phoning, so not answering must've had another reason behind it. To call it a disappointment after going through all the trouble to meet her, was to say nothing. Unable to locate her, he switched to number 2 on his list of Avenue's associates, which necessitated his return to Europe. At the back of his mind, he didn't oppose the idea of leaving Canada as soon as possible.

On the way to the airport Kevin couldn't stop wondering where the hell his appointee had abruptly disappeared to. Was Mrs. Dooling really a bait that got him into trouble the moment he landed in Canada? Suzy, Dooling - both worked for the late Avenue. Kevin tried to connect the dots.

The fate of the poor lady became known quite soon. She was busy being dead, killed by two shots from a handgun with a silencer in the crafty hand of a biker in a tinted helmet that came by her car when she was parking near the restaurant where she was supposed to meet Kevin.

The entire episode was recorded by the cameras in the parking lot, and that was the first thing shown to Kevin when he was apprehended by the Toronto police in the airport on the way back to London. They even slow-motioned the recording for Kevin so that he could see vividly each shot, gun's recoil, woman's head jerking back and blood dripping from each wound. Being handcuffed at the passport control was another nightmare that Kevin hadn't seen coming.

"What can you say about that, Mr. Lancaster?" Undoubtedly meant to be a punchline, they paused and enlarged the shoes worn by the biker, which were identical to Kevin's loafers. "We know you solicited this meeting! Why did you kill her?" The police interrogator looked menacing for pretense or for real.

Well done, Kevin - beaten, framed, soon fired, if my bosses hear about this flop. Kevin contemplated the situation from a whole new perspective.

The officer obviously didn't care much about Kevin missing his flight. He had his prime suspect. In fact, Kevin's leaving so abruptly after the murder further implicated him in something he hadn't done.

Clearing this would take time. Kevin had had a feeling that something must've happened. Now he knew what. From a victim of an assault, he swiftly turned into a murder suspect. What a day!

The meeting in Paris with Richard's deputy for Europe, second on the list of people whom Kevin planned to question, was postponed indefinitely.

Chapter 7
Call for help

So much for having the keys for two cars, if I couldn't put my nose out. Nor could I run. My leg was killing me each time I tried to stand. It wasn't the first time I'd been in this kinda situ, but the previous were (counter-) planned and dealt with by Arthur. Now I was on my own.

One flight down I saw a room that looked like an office. I crawled in. The door's opening allowed me to control the stairs, and that was what I needed. I decided to hold my defense from here.

I took the cellphones out. One was blocked with a fingerprint, and I didn't have time nor energy to crawl back to the corpse and cut a finger. The other one was an old Nokia. At least here I had some luck, as it functioned without a password.

So far, no movement on the stairs.

I moved closer to the window that offered a vista over the parking lot. Four cars were parked, and people were disembarking from two cars that had probably just arrived.

The wounded guy waited for them. Some proverb I had heard stated that an attack was the best defense. Having them all disposed in front of me just like that invited action. I opened the old wooden window, took a quick aim, and pulled the trigger. One-two-three.

I hit some fucker – the shriek of a wounded animal corroborated that, as he retreated quickly to hide behind the electrical substation on the verge of the parking space. The rest took shelter behind the cars. Although the area looked deserted, I hoped someone might hear the shots and come see what was up or call the police.

Now they'd move slowly. I noticed all the cars, apart from their unique number, bore in the end 23 and 93 - identifying the districts in Russia where they were registered.

I prayed for international calls to be open and maybe someone heard my prayer. With everything recorded in cell phone memories these days, I hardly remembered any numbers, but David's was among the few that I did.

Answer, goddammit! The phone was ringing, but David seemed reluctant to answer a call from an unrecognized number. Or maybe seeing the Russian number, he thought someone finally was making a ransom call and was readying himself for the moment. Just my speculations.

David didn't answer. Another major hope was blown.

My wife wasn't the right person to call for a brisk biz conversation when I had been missing for a few weeks.

By elimination, this left Sasha. Thank God, my brother picked up!

"That's me, brother. Just listen. I got hold of a cell phone for the first time in weeks. Please, listen carefully and if it disconnects, please return to this number. I was held hostage somewhere in Russia in the region with 23 and 93 car plates, check it on the internet, that's what I see on the cars here. And the docs of two goons read "Novorossiysk" for their home town. I'm in a building, encircled by armed men who'll storm it any minute." I knew my brother was all ears and wouldn't bother to interrupt me for silly questions.

I continued. "I'll try to fend them off for a while, but I doubt it'll last. These are some rogue gangsters and not the authorities, so I believe we have a chance the officials would want to intervene, if not for me, maybe for the sake of their 'order.' We do have connections. I think it could be helpful to contact Arthur's ex-army commander. I haven't spoken with him in ages and he might just not pick up the phone, but he's an FSB general and can handle this quickly."

I dismissed a quick thought about whether I really preferred to be in the hands of Russian authorities more than in those of their mafia. Not now. I had a situation to handle.

Seeing some skirmish outside, I made another two shots. This time they returned fire from their hiding places, their bullets smashing the remains of the glass in the window.

"Are you alright?" My brother was still on the line and extremely worried, judging by the tone of his voice.

"So far. And by the way, contacting local police may help too. See what you can do."

"Stay safe, brother. I'm on it." Sasha wouldn't waste time. But neither would the prospective assailants.

Chapter 8
Call for action

A call from a Canadian lawyer advising that Kevin was detained and suspected in murdering Mrs. Dooling catapulted David from literal slumber into action mode. He couldn't outsource tasks anymore. With Kevin bogged down in that imbroglio, he'd need to explore Suzy's thread himself. The urge and drive felt rejuvenating.

Kevin's mishaps and the murder of Richard's HR director cast a new light on the entire architecture of the events. *We are digging in the right direction,* thought David, while trying to figure how to approach Fabian – Richard's Deputy for Europe -- without endangering him and himself.

Paying an unannounced visit was tempting, but David decided against it.

First things first. He needed someone to prepare the ground and make sure Fabian remained there alive until David arrived to see him.

Who could be better than Simon, David's and Michael's old crony from the uni, serving some years in the French Legion in Africa and now living in Paris and operating a delivery biz? David dined with him regularly when visiting France and likewise when Simon was in London.

Bearing in mind the possibility of their devices being penetrated, David went downstairs, beckoned his driver, and asked for his cell phone. He left the building and reclined on the old oak in the inner yard of their London office, while on the watch-out that nobody would bother him. Most precautions are a waste of effort; however, those that work become critical.

"Hey, Simon, it's me." David counted on his friend recognizing his voice.

"Hi, David. Do you have a new number?" Simon's thick baritone conveyed the sense of a big man on the other end of the line. And big, almost two meters tall, he was.

"No, borrowed a cell from my employee. We might be screened here and I'm calling because I need your help with something."

"Wait a sec, I'll connect the earphones in case I need to write something down." Simon went straight to business.

"About Arthur's death and Misha's disappearance you know. Now, as soon as we started to look in Suzy's direction -- the bitch who did it -- we encountered active resistance. So active that Kevin -- do you know the guy?"

"No."

"Anyhow, he was beaten and framed for murder in Canada. He was supposed to meet one of Richard Avenue's, the late businessman I told you about, executives. She was killed instead of meeting Kevin. Kevin wasn't even given a chance to make it to the meeting. I need to meet Fabian Trimulinas, Richard's number two for Europe. But if I make my intention known, I'm afraid someone might attempt thwarting it. Can you arrange the meeting? Maybe even bring him here to London? I'd know how to protect him here."

"Sounds like you are in some real shit. I'll see what I can do. Send to my WhatsApp his contacts and details."

"*Merci*, Simon. Knew I could count on you."

I was rubbing my hands in apprehension when a few minutes later a photo of the postmortem arrived back from Simon: Fabian was happily dead for over two weeks now.

Chapter 9
<u>In the division</u>

"Kevin, Kevin, Kevin," the police officer was sarcastically melodramatic. "What an impressive specimen you are: seventeen years in Scotland Yard, eight years as a security advisor. Do you expect me to believe that such an experienced wolf as yourself can be tricked by some taxi driver, driven to nowhere, beaten and dropped off?"

"Yes, a big blunder on my part, but that's how it was." Kevin cherished hope that this misunderstanding wouldn't last long.

"And you don't know where they left you?" A broad smile on the interrogator's face showed he didn't believe it for a minute.

"Listen, Sir, you may believe it or not, but collecting or corroborating alibis was the least of my concerns right after being battered and abandoned in some suburb. If I'm such a wise guy, as you make of me, I'd come up with a better cover story. If you'd just check the location of my cell phone, you'd know I'm telling the truth. Please, bear with me. You can also try to find this guy, Mark, who picked me up on the road. He was driving a Black Chevrolet and he was heading to… What was it? York, I think."

Maybe Kevin did strike him as somewhat sincere or maybe his police duty to verify alternative versions prevailed, but he finally appeared attentive.

"For someone severely beaten you look pretty much intact. We'll check it, of course, but you might as well be more forthcoming with the purpose, chronology, and possible motives for killing a citizen seemingly uninvolved in anything. Why would someone want to rough you up, huh? Why come all the way to Canada to meet a lady you claim you haven't met before? I didn't hear any sound explanation regarding this. You are hiding something from us, for sure. And remember if your story crumbles, you are in deep shit, whatever glorious past you may have."

"It will hold, because that's what indeed happened." Kevin released a sigh of relief. "Please, try to find this biker who killed her. Believe me, it wasn't me. Don't waste your time. Surely, there might be a connection between two guys beating me and someone killing Mrs. Dooling. As to my purpose in meeting her, I already explained – I just hoped she'd be able to cast light on some former colleague. Maybe hook me up with someone. That's it." Kevin wasn't authorized to share the specifics of their internal investigation with any other authority. That was their corporate code of conduct. Maybe mafia style, but Kevin belonged to the system.

Irritated with complications of a seemingly already solved murder, the officer beckoned a constable to take Kevin back to the detention cell.

Chapter 10
Surrender?

Having connections in Russia gave me hope that local authorities would be competent enough to locate me. However, only a few Russians would openly admit knowing me in person; for too long I was viewed as sort of an unannounced enemy of the state there. I knew Sasha would pass along all the available details, so now it was just a question of time whether a rescue would come before the assailants managed to get their hands on me. That they would attempt, I had no doubt. I wasn't Rambo to be able to fend off the seven armed men that had disembarked from the cars.

Seven? Two more cars had just entered the parking lot with more fighters. I could only clearly see the drivers. They looked trained, commando-like. Apparently, they knew what was going on, so they put their cars sideways as a shield and took immediate cover, in case I tried to shoot.

From the "office" I could see only the front territory, but by this time I had no doubt that at least some of them had made their way around the building. And who knows, maybe more cars were in the back?

Wired and scared, I swept my sweaty forehead. The tension was rising, as I knew the storm was nigh.

Doesn't matter how many times you've been in life-threatening situations, the knowledge that maybe just a moment separates you from the unbeing makes it fateful. If I were to die today, I'd feel relieved. I would hardly make it into the annals of history -- not as someone glorious, heroic or benevolent, that is -- but I had accomplished a thing or two, achieved most of my goals and had some fun and happy moments to reminisce about.

And still I wanted to live. I was ready to give up on many things just to be around a little longer.

God, help me. I'll use my wealth and clout for greater good. I was bidding goodbye, but at the same time praying to stay alive.

Call it intuition, telepathy, or sixth sense, I realized someone was on the stairs. I crawled to the door and took aim at the stairwell, afraid even to blink.

A second, two, three, I saw them and pulled the trigger. It was a hit and my target fell back.

I heard curses, not the shriek of an injured man. He probably wore a vest and I had hardly hurt him.

I hurled a chair onto the stairs and it was immediately riddled from four or five barrels. If I had a grenade, it could help. But I didn't. Faced with such overwhelming opposition, I started to regret making my move today.

Maybe they read my thoughts, as someone just below suggested, "Vorotavich, resistance is pointless. We've got you. If you wanna die – fine -- we are here to help; but if survival still interests you, surrender and we'll prolong your misery for a while."

Where did they find this smart ass? I asked myself this rhetorical question, while my mind meandered trying to encompass the odds and the situation.

I wasn't in a bargaining position and they knew it. Their proposal made sense. There was no way anyone would come to my rescue before they got hold of me.

Obviously, killing me was their less-preferred option, even though they probably figured I had killed two of theirs. If they wanted me dead, they wouldn't negotiate.

A sharp shooter I wasn't, but I knew a thing or two about haggling!

"Hey, listen you down there. The next one that comes up, I'll shoot in the face not in the chest, so you might as well finish my misery now. Just come and try! I'm not going into captivity again. If you want something from me, you tell me now."

They fell silent, probably contemplating what I had said or maybe consulting someone. After all, their boss would hardly spearhead an operation involving live fire. I doubted my bravado would impress them; however, it paused their assault and let me drag some time. Buying time was all I wanted at this point.

"Mikhail, you'll find out what we want in our VIP guest jacuzzi," the negotiator chuckled and with him the rest of his crew. "Now, out, or we'll be coming up!"

Shit, I had hoped it'd take them longer. Not for surrender did I go through all the trouble. But what could I do? I could neither run nor repel them. I wrote, *"I've no choice but surrender. Still alive"* and sent it to Sasha, then deleted text and call history, turned it off, and put the phone into the drawer.

"Alright, I'm coming out." Perhaps, my prayers and desperation had finally reached the higher powers, as I heard a distinct siren.

Chapter 11
Call for help

The new frustration of David's attempts caused him to panic. Whoever they were up against was a step or two ahead in everything.

The sudden turnabout was just too good to be true. Sasha's call and update that Misha was alive, although in great jeopardy, was the best news in weeks, if not months.

It took less than a few seconds to produce from his phone's memory the telephone number of Arthur's army commander. And few more were spent on finding a short notice in Russian about his appointment to deputy chief of FSB. Exactly what David needed.

He dialed.

"Allo," a metallic-like timbre so associated with the stereotypes of KGB (now FSB) generals. Accustomed to lots of things in this life, David nonetheless shuddered.

"Anton Stepanovych, this is David Zabbana speaking, a friend and colleague of Mikhail Vorotavich. You might remember that your former subordinate Arthur Slotski, who worked as our chief of security, introduced us." David spoke in Russian, not pretending to conceal his accent, and knew he needed to be concise; otherwise, the general would disconnect a call from someone unknown.

"Arthur is dead."

"True, but Mikhail is still alive, kidnapped and kept captive in Krasnodar Krai of the Russian Federation. He's in great peril, but I hope you can help."

"Who's holding him? Have you submitted a formal complaint?" The general didn't sound too enthusiastic.

Fucking formalists. David hated these places, where procedures seemed more important than essence.

"Dear Anton Stepanovych," David felt for a sec as if he was writing a letter to Santa Claus. "We found out Misha's location only a few minutes ago. He attempted to escape and is now under siege in a remote building somewhere in that area. I have a phone number he called from to track his exact location. Whatever is necessary to comply with the procedures will be done. I promise. However, unless someone scrambles to his rescue, which by the way is the prime duty of every law enforcement agency, it might be too late. Now maybe you can still save his life." David tried to put as much urgency and conviction as he could into his trembling voice.

A pause on the other end of the line elongated beyond what David expected. Fidgeting, David held his breath, anticipating the general's reply.

"I'm giving the telephone to someone here, give him all the details. I'll be calling meanwhile to the head of Krasnodar FSB."

Yes! David yelled silently in his mind. Relieved, he told the anonymous listener about Misha's call, the cellular phone number he had called from, and other details that Sasha had briefed him on.

These guys were serious. He had no doubt they'd look into it.

Sasha entered the office meanwhile, as they'd agreed it would be better to stick together in these critical moments and share ideas on what else could be done.

"On the way here, I called Alexey Korzhun, you know the prime shareholder of Prosto Proso, as I remember he has a large silo or facility on the banks of Kuban River in the region and assumingly a large security force. Told him the situ and he promised to help. He has connections with chief of the police and others in the region." Sasha shared his updates.

"Alright, FSB and Korzhun. Who else?"

"Options are multiple." Sasha was thinking out loud. "We know, at least Misha does, three or four members of Duma, some industrialists and ministers, but these are longer shots, not suitable for immediate care. What do you think?"

"Agree." David tried to imagine in his mind the architecture of their connections in Russia. "Do you think they'd really try to help or would they rub their hands together in anticipation of getting rid of Misha? He's not exactly their hero, with his support of independent Ukraine."

"Yeah, such a thought also crossed my mind. But what else can we do? We can't possibly ask a foreign power to intervene in Misha's favor on Russian soil. Hell, if we had more time, I'm sure we could arrange a fair liberation squad from our own security, but they won't make it to Krasnodar earlier than within a few hours to a day. That's too late."

"We need someone on the ground immediately!" David arrived at a conclusion. "It would take hours from London, but should be faster from Georgia. I'll ask Rezo to go there now. And if we could somehow organize satellite surveillance, it'd be even better. Alas."

Rezo was chief of their Caucasus operations, a junior partner in business, very loyal to Misha.

They didn't even need to ask: as soon as he heard that Misha had disclosed his location, Rezo suggested he'd hire a plane to get there forthwith and bring some "brave guys" with him.

Sasha and David knew exactly whom he was talking about.

Chapter 12
A Detour

Kevin's head was exploding. Thank god, not literally, but it felt that way. The Canadians wanted answers and so did Kevin, except he was still the main suspect. The journey that was supposed to be a walk in the park had turned into a nightmare.

Kevin couldn't sleep or eat and, knowing the police tricks of placing undercover cops into the cell to procure info, he tried not to socialize. Not that he had anything to hide. Instinctively.

David found Kevin in a state of complete disarray, physically and emotionally exhausted. However, David wasn't too compassionate. Annoyed by Kevin's negligence of basically stepping into every trap laid for him and by the need to come to his rescue, as their principle was not to leave their people in trouble in the "battlefield," he felt he needed to be closer to Misha, who had briefly resurfaced, but instead flew all the way to Canada. He and Sasha had done all they could and now was maybe the hardest part – to sit and wait for news, biting nails from anxiety. In a way, a detour to Canada was an alternative for restless fidgeting back in the office.

"Kevin, I've arranged for the best legal team possible. Cost us a small fortune, but I hope you'll be released soon, whether under a bail or unconditionally."

"Thanks, David, appreciate the effort. Didn't mean to fuck up this way. Thinking it over here in detention, it was neatly organized though. Ruthless, but smart."

"Yeah, I know. Misha called, I'm sure you'll be cheered to know. And he's not on the honeymoon with Suzy, as you can imagine. He's in trouble in Russia. We are trying to organize his rescue." Jetlagged, David sounded uninspired.

"Holly shit, this is terrific news!" Kevin tried to disengage for a moment from his own imbroglio.

"Yeah, except it was a few hours ago when he was encircled by some goons, and we haven't heard from him or about him since. Anyway, don't expect much from the Canadian police. Those who waited for you and whacked Mrs. Dooling have probably long left Canada, but who knows. We need to find out the connections between your adversaries here, Misha's captors in Russia, Suzy, and god knows who else. These all look like links of the same chain. You keep yourself safe, but you have a task: Try to see what the police manage to gather." David wondered if the police were eavesdropping on this conversation. Referring to his formal education and membership in the Israeli Bar, David had introduced himself as a lawyer, hoping that would let him speak with the "client" without fear of police listening.

David continued: "Cooperate with them." He winked to mean *not really*. "Maybe they'll find the cab, the assailants who picked you up, or some evidence at the murder scene. Try to be hands on, even as a suspect. Now that you have the best criminal lawyers involved, I'm sure you'll be treated with more respect."

"Thanks for everything, David." Kevin knew that in situations like this their corporate holding acted as a family. *Mafia style*, as he had dubbed it a while ago. "I'll hold on as long as it's necessary and try to follow the developments at close distance. I'll cooperate." He returned the wink.

"Take care. Hope you don't need me here any longer." David bowed away with a blank expression - his thoughts and heart were a thousand miles away.

Misha was the living spirit behind the entire crew. Hearing that he was back and fighting enthused everyone, Kevin included.

During the next interrogation, he planned to play the hunter, not the prey.

Chapter 13
<u>When bullets fly</u>

Change of plans, baby. Forget about coming out. The siren was the best sound I could imagine.

Those waiting for me to come out understood it too.

"Mikhail, I count to ten. You are either out, or we will grill your ass first and face the consequences later."

I let him count to eight and said, "Don't fire, I'm coming out." I was bent on using every tactic to win every second. I hurled another chair into the stairwell. The machine gun went into action.

"Are you gonna kill me?" I tried to express sincere fear.

"You are not a chair. Drop the gun and put your hands behind your head. Stop fucking with us, cunt." The speaker grew impatient. The siren was practically here; they should switch attention to that. I would. I saw three armored buses of OMON, the police storm unit, or maybe of FSB, as they didn't have insignia, entering the parking lot one after another.

Wearing all black, the squad spilled out of the buses and spread around like cockroaches, occupying the same ground as another troop maybe half an hour earlier. The last one who disembarked was their commander with the loudspeaker in his hands.

He didn't waste time. With arrogant tone and bossy bearing, he announced: "Everyone who's inside the building and nearby, drop your weapons and come out with your arms raised above your head. The resistance is futile; you are surrounded. Any careless movement will be met with live fire."

We had just changed roles with the captors. I hoped they didn't have orders to liquidate me if worse came to worst. I doubted they were kamikaze, ready to sacrifice themselves just to kill me.

The tense silence stilled the air. The last thing I wanted was to get stuck in the middle of a gunfight. I was hesitating between lying down the lowest I could or dropping myself out of the window from the second floor. However, knowing how trigger-happy and wired these guys were, I thought it was extremely risky, and I could absorb a couple of bullets even before reaching the ground. I believed that by firing even a single shot, the entire place would explode with the fire exchange on both sides.

Fuck. I saw a shadow on the stairs and gripped the gun firmly, not wanting but ready to shoot. The assailants were coming my way, but it seemed more retreating than with the intention to get me.

Not so easy. I spoke up, yelling out the window without showing myself. "This is Mikhail. I'm on the second floor. Please, don't shoot. I'm the victim, kept captive here. A heavily armed troop is retreating to my position using the stairs."

They heard me well. The commander paused for a minute and then gave some order to the subordinates around, as the squad came into motion flanking the building from both sides.

Only a few seconds passed, as I heard a shriek. "Here they are!" and bullets started to hiss all around, but mostly on the rear side.

Pity they were stubborn. OMON or Alpha (whatever special operations unit had just arrived) would wipe them out. I hoped not all of them, as I wanted to know who was behind those assholes.

My relief, if indeed I felt it for a brief moment, was premature. All of a sudden, I heard the stomp of feet coming up the stairs again, accompanied by bullets. Many of them.

Shit, they gonna ram into me. The thick of the gunfight was rapidly approaching.

I fired a few bullets into the stairwell to make them cautious on approach and then crawled as fast as I could towards the window. Even with my back to them, I felt them getting close.

I turned around just in time to shoot at a figure entering the room and then pulled myself up and out of the window, yelling for my life, "Don't sho-o-o-ot!" I fell down to the ground, trying to cushion my landing with my arms and then rolling sideways.

I felt an acute pain, but not from the shots. It was my arm – now undoubtedly broken too.

I was not the only one. I had barely stopped rolling as another man with a Kalach in his hands jumped down, and then another.

As soon as one of them tried to stand and run, he was shot in the head by four commandos approaching and encircling us.

"Drop your weapons, hands up!" One of them shouted.

I hurled my gun and raised my left hand, lying on my back.

"My leg and arm are broken. I can't stand," I yelled back.

The other guy stood with his hands up, his AK-47 left on the ground.

While handcuffing the guy who had jumped after me, an officer nodded in my direction and announced, "It's him."

Chapter 14
Kevin the hunter

Kevin didn't like lawyers. Ever since joining the police force, he and the boys had worked hard to put criminals behind bars, while those slick bastards just existed to derail their efforts and make a luxurious living out of it no less.

Now he needed one. Or maybe he didn't. In Kevin's opinion, his testimony was so easy to cross-check: find the cab, the place where he was beaten, triangulate his cell phone -- not something extraordinary, but locals kept dragging on these things.

So what if the biker wore the same boots? You can't keep someone locked away because of some bloody insignificant match or circumstantial evidence. Clearly, it was engineered in advance, but who would think he'd be stuck trying to prove his innocence for a week. Exactly – to prove his innocence. That was how he felt. Toronto police didn't bother to substantiate his guilt beyond the tape from the underground parking lot. Ah, and his leaving the country "hastily," as they put it.

These and other thoughts Kevin, simmering for a long while, was unloading onto Jules Praktikant, Esquire.

"A good lawyer can tear these allegations apart. I'm sick of this 'the shoes, the shoes, the shoes' tune of each interrogator." Kevin sounded and looked fed up.

"They try to break you, to wear you down. You should know these tricks. Hold on and I hope I can get you released under bail." Jules wasn't particularly impressed by Kevin's complaints, as he heard similar ones every day.

Most of his clients were "innocent." For a few days. Only to confess in a few more. After spending twenty years in the legal biz, Praktikant didn't care. A judicial truth and a factual one were not the same beast. Often the opposite. This Kevin could be a killer or a victim; it changed nothing in Jules' practical approach to get him out of custody. That was what he was paid for, and generously so.

"This is what you gonna do," he was instructing his new client like hundreds of others before him, only a barely noticeable trace of French accent betraying his mother tongue. "You don't talk in the cell."

"I know that."

"I'll try to negotiate a bail with the superintendent, whom I've known since he was a rookie in the street patrol." He certainly tried to impress the client with his connections. "Also, I'll try to find the guy who gave you a lift and the place where you were thrown out of the cab. The police may lack manpower for this. I have the budget and best private detectives, who can do it efficiently. At this stage we just need a single piece of external evidence to corroborate your story and thus shake the police's suspicions about you. If it exists, we'll find it. You can count on us, Mr. Lancaster."

A bail was better than the cell, no questions asked. This Jules dude laid good perspectives, but could he deliver? Hopefully.

While escorted to the next interrogation, Kevin bore in mind David's request, waiting for an opportunity. He walked down the corridor somewhat inspired.

The same room again. He hated it. How many times he had played the other role, that of an interrogator, in a similar room in London. There were probably thousands, if not millions, of similar interrogation rooms scattered around the globe, where smart or cruel -- or both -- investigators any given minute tried to extort confessions from the suspects. Here he was a suspect on foreign turf.

Inspector Galvany was clearly pissed. Or made himself look that way. Kevin had seen him that way before and it meant nothing good.

"What is it?" The Inspector dropped on the table a small photo containing an image of the hammer and sickle.

"What? Is it a history quiz? Looks like the symbol of the USSR, if I remember correctly." Kevin frowned.

"No shit, it is. What was it doing at the crime scene?" Galvany started the pressure.

"How the hell do I know? I've never been to the crime scene!"

"You are a fucking liar. And don't even think your top-notch lawyer will get you out of here."

Galvany's phone rang. He darted his gaze at the incoming number and after a moment of hesitation went out of the room to take the call.

Kevin wasted no time opening the file left on the table and quickly leafing through it. There was a risk, but those who don't take them never drink champagne. That was a saying in Russian Kevin had picked up from Misha at the time. Most of the materials were related to Kevin: intelligence report, background record, her majesty's police answer to the Canadian inquiry -- nothing Kevin didn't know about his old self.

The interesting, even bizarre, part contained a list of organizations connected with Marxist theory, Communism, and similar extreme stuff. *What the hell? How could this shit be connected?*

There was also a search warrant related to Ms. Gertrude Ninette, Lawrence Avenue, Toronto, and signed formal enquiries regarding some non-profit organizations: "The Proletarian Union of Oil Industry of Canada" and "Labor Solidarity Force."

Kevin had hoped they would have a few more suspects, but the file reflected none.

Not that he particularly worried that Galvany would notice him peeping into the police documents now that he'd finished, but Kevin made sure to close the case file well before the door reopened and an even more agitated interrogator stormed in.

"Take him to the cell," he yelled back to a warden, then grabbed the folder and exited the room first.

Chapter 15
In the hospital

Thank God, it was a hospital. A shabby, backwater one, but still a medical institution. For someone my age, I felt I'd frequented hospitals more than I should have.

I didn't remember how we had gotten here, nor what had happened on the way. My life chronology was too patchy, as these "black holes" in my memory had multiplied lately.

I totally collapsed into oblivion. My injuries and utmost effort to try to escape had discharged all my batteries.

I came to my senses after, what, a few hours? A few days? I didn't know.

My aching body seemed to send pain signals from at least a dozen places on my body map. I tried to stand, but crumbled on the floor, then pulled myself back up into the bed.

Wow, I don't feel my feet. I did feel sedated and had clearly overestimated my current capabilities in an attempt to stand up.

I looked closely at all the bandages. My right leg in a cast, right arm bandaged, a big bandage on the chest, close to the upper left side, plasters all over the body. Nothing excessive, yet I couldn't walk.

All of a sudden, the door opened and some medic, judging by his light green scrubs, came in.

"Oh, our patient is awake," he said matter-of-factly. "How do we feel?" He was obviously addressing me under this "we."

I thought I had seen two men standing by the door when he opened it. *Guards? Wardens?*

"Feeling not exactly ready for the Olympics, but tolerable. What's with my leg, doc?"

"Regret to say – we needed to amputate it."

"What?!" I reached nervously down, trying to feel what was under the cast. The leg was there. Then I reached for the other and grabbed empty air! To call it a shock would be a gross understatement. I felt dizzy and fainting.

"But how could you? I didn't agree to this." I gathered myself together and struggled to understand how come I was missing a leg.

"It was a lifesaving emergency. There was an infection spreading: It was a 'cut or die' situation. You got injured while trying to escape, so we assumed you'd choose life. And even if we assumed otherwise, we were obliged to save you."

I felt like crying. Something long forgotten. *Misha the invalid, a creep.* Never could've imagined myself in such a situation. Dead – yes, and many times before. But crippled?! *Take it as it is, don't break down.* I was frantically convincing myself.

The doc sensed my inner suffering and seemed attentive for a moment until I regained my composure. Or maybe he pretended to.

"Tell me, please, I saw two guys by the doors when you entered." I tried to change the subject to come to grips with my current status.

"Yes, what about them?" The doc became disinterested again.

"Am I in custody? Are they here to protect me or prevent my escape?" Too shocked to come up with something smart, I went for the straightforward approach.

"Um, I don't know the status exactly, but I'll let them know you're conscious. You can clarify with them or their superior, who put them there."

"Thanks."

Changing one incarceration for another wasn't exactly my purpose.

As the doc opened the door to exit, a solid punch hurled him back into the room.

Chapter 16

Was somebody looking for Suzy?

Waiting for takeoff, David was leaving Canada with heavy thoughts sitting on his mind. After the shock and despair that had prevailed during the first days after Misha's disappearance, they'd mapped out the directions and started to act along them, but all their moves seemed stalled, compromised, or openly obstructed. Moreover, each of their moves was known to the other side, whoever it was, and sabotaged. Pondering over the identity of the mole, David inevitably drifted towards Suzy. For too long she had been in Misha's inner circle and able to plant surveillance, bugs, and whatever nasty spying stuff there existed. She was the mole and the enemy. Betrayal of others couldn't be ruled out lightly, but didn't make much sense. After the lesson with the American banker who had worked for him in the past and switched sides, Michael meticulously made sure all of his close people were content, and paid special personal attention to each. Maybe not totally foolproof, but David felt they had a reliable nucleus.

What's up with Misha? David bit his nails in anxiety. Misha had resurfaced on his own and it was a shame they'd done so little to help him.

After spending time held captive by the Seven, David had hoped their adventurous part of life was over. Yet, they'd somehow entered something far more dangerous, where they didn't even know who the opponents were.

Oh, how he missed Boris, for his cynical but somehow placating remarks -- and Arthur, for his silent assurance that when shit hit the fan, there was someone to take it abreast.

David was a team player, not a loner. He was always wondering whether to finally hang up the gloves and trade his biz for regular family life.

Thank God, they have sat phones on Dreamliner. The last thing David wanted was to miss news from their Russian teams. He had wrapped up his Canada visit in less than three hours after arriving.

The silence from a place where things were supposed to be boiling was unnerving, frightening. They had tried to contact the General again, but his line was silent too.

Vaguely registering the events preceding the takeoff and commencement of the flight, David was immersed in thoughts. Like the plane, he acted on autopilot until someone grabbed him by the sleeve and pulled slightly.

"Mr. Zabbana, I think you might be looking for me." A lady wearing a broad straw hat pulled down, so that it covered most of her face, on purpose no doubt, half whispered, "Come."

"What is it, some silly spy movie?" and then "Suzy?!" David recognized her all of a sudden and made a great effort not to shout. He had just thought about her and here she was. It was like a miracle -- or call it a bad surprise. David still couldn't suppress his outrage.

"Shhh. Come, there is an empty row in the back."

She looked friendly and complacent, but David didn't forget for a second that she had killed Arthur and kidnapped Misha.

"Why should I come with you? I'll make sure you are arrested the moment we touch down." David made up his mind, baffled at first by her foot-in-the-door tactic.

"No, you won't, at least not after you hear me out. Don't be afraid. I've limited options to kill you aboard." Suzy was almost charming, probably imagining in her sick mind those "limited options."

"All right then. What the hell." David managed to cool himself down, as he too had limited options of getting her arrested before landing.

Looking more like a perfect couple rather than a deadly woman and a distressed millionaire caught off guard, they occupied an empty row, Suzy grabbing a seat by the window, leaving the aisle to David, thus stressing that he could leave at any time.

"Listen, David, I was wrong. Terribly so." Suzy took the bull by the horns without any small talk.

"You bet you were, and you'll pay dearly for it." David didn't attempt to conceal his disdain.

"You don't get me. I was sure Arthur had killed Richard, and I held him and his boss Misha responsible for Richard's death. Richard was my brother."

"What? Richard was your brother?! And why would you stupidly assume that Misha would want him killed?" David asked exasperatedly, still a little surprised because they'd always thought she and Richard were lovers. As far as he remembered, their intel about Avenue never mentioned any sister.

"I told you, I was wrong. Michael was the last man he met before dying on the plane. Richard was poisoned. Richard was wary and worried to meet Misha, describing him as a dangerous person. When my brother died, I vowed to avenge his death and I had no doubt it was Misha, delegating the task to Arthur. Oh, for how long did I relish my revenge, sleeping with the enemy, until I finally pulled it off, only to find out that I was wrong all along." Suzy's regret was sincere, and yet her fury for revenge was rekindled.

"You daft cunt." David felt no mercy, as Arthur was dead and Misha maybe hanging by a hair.

In any other circumstances, Suzy would probably hurt anyone saying these words to her, but she sadly agreed. "True. After I handed Vorotavich to the Russians, all sorts of pieces started to fall into place depicting a totally different picture. At some stage I couldn't ignore it anymore." Suzy waved off the stewardess offering refreshments, impatient to continue.

David, thirsty, slowly pondering over Suzy's story, stopped the stewardess instead to get some water.

"So, what did you find out?"

"After a while rummaging through Richard's stuff, I found in his papers-- but even more, in emails -- that he was in contact with some 'liberty' or 'proletarian union' or whatever. Then I checked the passengers' list from his last flight and discovered one of those 'proletarians,'" Suzy pronounced it with an unveiled hatred, "sitting right near him. Then, there was more, and my confidence in the new direction grew. At some point, only too late, I understood that Misha and Arthur had probably had nothing to do with my brother's death! You wouldn't believe it, but were I not hating him for something he hadn't done, I would have loved Arthur." Suzy was pouring out this stuff as if at a confession. She sobbed, for even her hardened heart wasn't one hundred percent immune to feelings.

It's just so idiotic. David didn't say it out loud. Arthur had risked his life so many times, for real reasons and under real threats, and it was unthinkable that he had been killed for some silly mistake by a self-pronounced female Sherlock Holmes.

But she wasn't finished yet.

"And then there was this strange clause in his will, bequeathing half of his estate to a Marxist....... Organization. This made ... "

David's satellite phone rang. He knew it was about Misha.

"Hi, David, we found him. There is a problem, though ..."

Chapter 17
Release

"Sign here. And here," the officer handed Kevin his belongings indifferently. "Always welcome back."

Kevin hated this humor, and his acquaintance with Toronto police force had been a nightmare, so he couldn't even leave them with a smile.

He left the police building with his lawyer, who wasn't exactly beaming with cordiality.

All businesslike, he equipped David with 1K Canadian dollars, a voucher for the hotel, and the keys for the rented car parked across the street in the parking lot.

"Take care, make sure not to violate the bail terms; otherwise it'll be hard to get you out again. Nothing stupid, please." He shook Kevin's hand.

"Thanks, sure." Kevin nodded.

However, his investigator's instinct had been burning inside him ever since he had leafed through Galvany's folder. He had been toying with a thought for a while.

He breathed some fresh air, distancing himself as soon as possible from the police, as if in fear they might reconsider his release. Keys in the ignition, radio on, he entered the address of the hotel into the navigation app. His wallet had been returned "thinner" from the police (most of the cash was stolen), his laptop and cell phone still in their custody – supposedly investigated.

Contemplating his further moves, Kevin stopped at the first appropriate store he saw on the way to the hotel. He grabbed a smart phone with pre-paid data and sim card and hurried away to his destination, paying in cash, so comfortably availed by his attorney, instead of the credit card to leave fewer "footprints."

Checking in and ordering room service took only a few minutes and Kevin felt he was back into biz.

He phoned the London office, trying to reach David or Sasha. No one was available, and none of them answered their mobiles. Something was going on in another part of the globe, something concerning Misha no doubt. Seeing his new, unfamiliar number, they'd probably chosen not to waste their time. Kevin wrote a short WhatsApp message to both of them, primarily to inform about his release, to advise his new temporary Canadian number, and to ask for further instructions.

In the meantime, his instincts screamed that the findings in the police station's files could be useful.

He Googled "The Proletarian Union of Oil Industry of Canada," "Labor Solidarity Force," and finally "Gertrude Ninette." The first two seemed interconnected: both were obscure non-profits using the same suppliers, powered by the same host provider, and using the services of the same web designer. The lady's name returned with no results. The organizations had socialistic inclinations, but otherwise offered nothing too suspicious, except maybe listing no physical addresses or contact data beyond Internet interface. His first impression changed rapidly once he entered his corporate secret database, partially available on the cloud. Both organizations appeared to be blacklisted by anti-money laundering authorities in Canada, US and EU, and both were suspected of terror activity and cybercrimes. Searching "Gertrude" still didn't produce any results.

Hmm... again some innocent veil hides quite a sinister activity, mused Kevin. He needed to check it out closely, except this time he didn't intend to jump in headlong. He hoped he'd exhausted his list of blunders for this trip.

He needed location, preparation, and reinforcement. Hoping to plan an operation or raid, he Skyped David.

Chapter 18
A few days earlier
<u>Preparations</u>

Rezo and a crew of six men -- more precisely beasts in men's guise -- arrived at the scene in the midst of the shooting exchange. Trying to understand what was going on and who was fighting whom, Rezo ordered his men to lay low on the hill overlooking an abandoned building to which Misha had been tracked.

"That's some fucking Tarantino movie, blyad," he told Givi with a sinister grin. "Now we are a new gang arriving in time to whack the winners just when they grab the loot."

Givi nodded, which neither confirmed nor denied whether he understood the allegory.

The fight beneath them was rapidly approaching resolution, with those equipped like special forces coming out with the upper hand. Intervening at this stage seemed stupid.

Once the commander of the uniformed dudes took off his assault mask, Rezo exclaimed, "Ha, that's no other but Major Timofeev. Alpha unit, FSB, my friends."

And then he saw Misha being lifted from the ground and put on the stretcher. *Is he alive?* A panicky thought crept in.

Not that Rezo liked FSB or thought his guys were inferior combatants -- it's just that assaulting an official Russian special unit meant they'd be hunted forever, even if they managed to snatch Misha from FSB's hands.

He signaled his troop to back away. Knowing in whose hands Misha was, they needed a more subtle operation. Misha's being under FSB's auspices didn't suggest anything promising or hospitable.

"Akhrik, take David and these cars," he pointed at the rented Lada and Niva "and follow the bus with 27 on its number plate, the one in which they placed Mikhail's stretcher. Do it professionally. Don't get too close, switch between the cars. I don't want them to spot a tail. We need to know where they'll be taking him."

After a short pause, he said, "You know what, Givi, go with them, just in case. Send the location once you find out where they transport Misha to."

There were not so many options: if Misha was alive, they'd take him either to FSB Medical Institute or to Krasnodar Central Hospital; if dead – to the city morgue. Rezo really hoped it would be one of the first two.

**

"What did I tell you?" He showed Ramaz his cellphone with a WhatsApp message from Givi saying "Krasnodar Central Hospital" about two hours after he and the others had left.

"We are on, guys. Let's get some action going."

They needed to act quickly, before the higher-ranking officers in the FSB chain of command decided what to do with such a sweet catch as Mikhail Vorotavich, notorious for his pro-Ukrainian and thus, some say, anti-Russian stance. Medical treatment and subsequent release were an option, but the chances weren't that high. Too many times Misha's interests had crossed with those pulling the strings in Russia and worldwide. They had him unexpectedly, but as soon as they realized what a lucky opportunity that was, they would think how to monetize it literally and virtually.

"Quick" meant Rezo couldn't count on reinforcements, but his six-man crew was worth a dozen. What he did need was a safe retreat, so he made a short drive to Krasnodar Airport to arrange permits for a private jet to land and wait for them at the airport that evening.

The tentative plan was shaping in his mind: different options weighed, questioned, refuted, or accepted. But - recognizance first.

He routed all his team to Krasnodar, where Misha was hospitalized. Upon arrival they first dispersed in pairs between cafes in the center to pretend holding business lunches, but staying within eye contact of each other. As Givi was both the best actor and had nerves of steel, he received the assignment to search through the hospital to see where Misha was, guarded or not, and desirably return with a film of the surroundings, while avoiding direct contact with anyone involved at this stage. Having his entire spy gear with him, the button-camera was attached to Givi's button-down in a matter of seconds.

***

You can't look like or pretend to be a passerby or a dog walker in such a busy place as the hospital. Givi entered the sliding doors and headed forward with the confident hurried pace of someone who knew where he was heading.

This peripheral hospital had only three buildings: two five-storied and one nine-storied. In half an hour he could pass through every floor, as he didn't want to ask anyone anything at this stage.

Soon he found what he needed. Passing by the doctors' room on the third floor, he saw a doctor exiting and leaving the door open. As soon as Givi noticed that the doc was waiting for the elevator, he decided to take a chance. Unnoticed, he entered the room, grabbed a white gown thrown casually on a chair, donned it, and rushed to the computer.

Typing "Vorotavich" didn't reveal anything. Cool and composed, he nonetheless had sweaty palms. Any second someone could enter. Givi peeped out and, seeing a still-empty corridor, made a second attempt, checking today's admissions.

Ah, there you are. He quickly pointed his camera button towards the screen to copy the info: "…A wounded man of above forty years old, brought for treatment by Alpha regiment of FSB, sustaining firearm injuries and …," Givi didn't read further. He just memorized *Intensive Care Unit 5, Building C.*

Half of his mission was accomplished. So far, so good. He swiftly left the room and headed straight to building C. The white gown was left where it was taken from.

***

Givi's luck took a deep dive once he got closer to the target. As soon as the elevator's doors opened at the fourth floor, hosting Unit Five, he was greeted coldly by an officer sitting at a table; at his sides were two guards in full gear, with their fingers on the triggers of assault rifles. "Your name and passport."

Givi had hoped he'd be able to walk through the floor, pass by, but stay clear of the guards. He wasn't prepared for such an encounter.

Displaying shock and surprise at the sight of armed guards should be natural; however, he tried as hard as possible to conceal a sudden sting of fright and panic while improvising how to proceed.

He didn't want to push it, but he didn't have a convincing story handy.

"Kh, khm, err... Umh, excuse me?" Givi stared blankly at the officer.

"Your name and documents." The officer's reply sounded automatic and impersonal.

"Oh, sure. Here. Mladen Stojanov." Givi produced his forged Bulgarian passport. "Is the proctologist ...err.... busy?"

The officer studied his passport with disinterest. The guards didn't jump or shoot him either. Yet, Givi felt wired, hoping his credentials were sufficiently professional to pass the scrutiny.

"A proctologist? This is an intensive care, tovarish." The officer put the passport on the table.

"Oh, sorry, I must've got out on the wrong floor," said Givi apologetically, but with a sigh of relief.

At that moment, the door behind the guards opened to let out a nurse pushing an empty wheelchair.

It was enough for Givi to see a long corridor with two more guards standing by the third or fourth room on the left. That glimpse was all he was looking for.

Givi grabbed his passport and turned back towards the elevator. *Ok, an officer and four guards from FSB special assault unit – maybe not something insurmountable, but not an easy opposition either.*

Givi needed to relay the layout to Rezo, and hoped he'd find a way other than an all-out assault.

Chapter 19
Anxiety

Rezo's updates outshone whatever important things Suzy had to tell. David excused himself to intake the info alone. Hearing that they were about to attempt to bring Misha home put the pressure up another notch. David became restless – probably the worst state to be in when on the plane, which offered limited options to quell the anxiety.

With his mind on what was happening in Kuban region, it took him a while to return to the conversation with Suzy. He felt it wasn't his business. If rescued, Misha should decide what to do with her.

Seeing her seated just a few rows away from him and watching his face intently, he approached Suzy again only to deliver his verdict.

"Listen, you've got us all into this mess and I really should report you upon landing. We were actually looking for you to find out whom you transferred Misha to, but now that we've found him, your info is of secondary importance. I hope Misha will be in the position to decide your fate. Our dialogue is not over, but I currently have more urgent matters to attend to. I suggest you stay put and let me know where to find you when needed."

Suzy reached into the inner pocket of her jacket. For a sec David didn't breathe, expecting her to produce anything from a pistol to a syringe with some poison, but instead her hand reappeared with a pen and a small notebook. She wrote the number on the page, tore it from the notebook, and gave it to David. *Just like meeting a girl in a club,* was a thought that crossed David's mind.

"Call me. I know how to get Misha out. I can undo it."

Too late, bitch. Who needs you now? David didn't nod or say a word. He just knew their conversation was to be continued. If she wanted to disappear again, she wouldn't have contacted him in the first place.

***

To distract himself from growing anxiety, David tried to busy himself with the matters at hand in descending priority. Seeing Kevin online on Messenger meant he was freed. David registered the obvious without giving it much of a thought. Still immersed in Rezo's report about Misha being treated under heavy FSB security protocol, he couldn't answer now.

First, he attempted to reach the FSB general who had intervened to free Misha from the kidnappers. David hoped to understand from him Misha's status in FSB's custody: whether he was a guest or a prisoner.

He didn't answer. Again. That wasn't the best sign. Misha always taught his men to assume the worst, and David usually agreed with that approach. Maybe the FSB dudes hadn't made up their minds yet how to treat Misha, since he had been discovered so unexpectedly on Russian soil.

During a conference call between himself, Rezo, and Sasha, they pretty much came to the same conclusion that they needed to snatch Misha out of Russia as soon as possible, for if FSB decided they wanted him kept, they would have zero chance to get him out.

Organizing a plane for Rezo wasn't a problem. They went for a wet charter, instead of using the group's jets, so as not to attract attention. They all agreed that the window of opportunity wouldn't be open forever. Maybe it was a matter of hours, maybe a day or two, but the presence of Rezo's group would be discovered by the authorities. Once known, their capabilities would be neutralized.

Rezo's last words, "No worries, everything's under control. We'll go in tonight," still reverberated in David's ears. Yeah, Rezo wasn't a bragging kid with bravado bigger than brains, but the delicacy of the operation hung in the air and was felt by all the participants of their impromptu consultation.

Together with the plane, they dispatched another security unit. Just in case.

It certainly wasn't the first time, and David hated those culminations where he could influence nothing and just needed to sit and wait, hoping others would deliver.

To alleviate the pressure, he Skyped Kevin back.

"Glad to see you out of the police station, pal." David managed to be cordial and sarcastic at the same time.

"Thank you, David." Kevin didn't feel comfortable to joke back to the superior, not after he had virtually fucked up in Canada.

"Missed your call. What's up?"

"Actually, there are some promising leads." Kevin updated David on his initial findings.

Hearing "Proletarian" and "Solidarity" for a second there, David had an acute feeling of *déjà vu*. He fell silent, trying to put his finger on it. It didn't pop up, and it irritated him. Kevin on the other side of the line played along and waited patiently until David had absorbed the information.

"Shit, this rings some bell.... Anyway, so what's your plan?" David let go and continued.

"Being a suspect, I might be followed. I think the leads are worth looking into and I'll need a small team here to explore it a little further. If you can authorize Greg and Silvinsky joining me here, we can check these leads out in a matter of days. I've charted it out."

"You've got them. Cut the bureaucracy short and get in touch with them directly to work out the logistics and timetable. Refer to my consent with everything you need; use Gina in the financial department. Just don't do anything stupid. I expected whatever, but not getting you out of the police station. That was a trap for beginners."

David was never into blaming and finding scapegoats; he was into solutions and what to do next. Mentioning Kevin's blunder should motivate him to try harder to improve his reputation. After all, Arthur's position remained vacant and everyone in the security section still viewed it as an opportunity.

Recalling Arthur immediately reminded him of Suzy. *There it is!* David's *déjà vu*, annoyingly sitting at the back of his head, finally materialized. *Holy shit, didn't Suzy tell me something about some Marxists, just before Rezo called? These Proletarian dudes must be from the same opera!*

Chapter 20
Going in

Audacity – that was the key to success. Using raw force would mean casualties, and Rezo didn't want any among his men, nor among FSB officers. Killing any of them would put him on the radar for years to come until they'd find him to square the score. Not that Rezo was afraid of confrontation; it just seemed unwise. Maybe a few years earlier, he'd have succumbed to the adrenaline and his hot blood and would have opted for a confrontational resolution; but now he was a commander of the group and a mature one.

However, excluding an exchange of fire as an option would also be stupid, since everyone involved on both sides was armed to the teeth, so he had his men prepared for any eventuality.

To their surprise, the first thing Rezo did after hearing out Givi's report and showing the recording of his button-camera to all, was taking two men with him to the nearest mall.

Wasting minimal time, they came out appearing to be different people wearing business suits and ties, however still with the firm tread of military men. Hiding holsters under the fancy suit jackets wasn't that much of a challenge, but it necessitated waiving the bulletproof vests.

The second thing was converting one of the hotel rooms into an impromptu make-up parlor. Wigs, mustaches, scars heavily, but not artificially so, camouflaged their real look. After all, they'd need to pose in front of the cameras.

As joking always improved spirits and morale, Rezo suggested remodeling Givi, who looked the most masculine of the bunch, with dense hair cover all over him, into a woman.

Holding out a red lipstick, Rezo ventured, "Hey Givi, how about a final touch for a fine disguise?"

Imaging the unimaginable, the entire crew almost pissed their pants laughing. Almost – except for Givi, of course, who didn't take well that kind of humor and was enraged.

"You idiots. What are you laughing at, ah? I'll show you a woman." He poured powder on Ahrik's head.

"Come on. Relax, man." The desired effect was achieved, and Rezo didn't want it going any further, neither towards an excessively humorous mood nor towards angry retorts. Frankly speaking, he regretted having no women on the team – there just were things that women were better at.

***

The minibus was silent all the way from the hotel to the hospital. Concentration, a sense of peril, and the importance of the mission all added to the air pressure.

They stopped two blocks away from the hospital, leaving the back-up team there, to walk the rest of the distance by foot, while the driver took the business-suited team to the hospital's parking lot.

Rezo, with a French mustache and a wig, flashed an FSB certificate at the hospital's entrance – not good enough for serious scrutiny, but sufficiently frightening for the parking guard, who saluted and rushed to open the gate.

They'd done a general rehearsal three times and now headed firmly towards the underground elevator. The first hurdle waited for them right behind the elevator's doors on the fourth floor.

The eyes of the three of them were on the small digital screen of the elevator, counting one, two, three, four. Instinctively, Rezo rechecked his Glock 18 under the jacket and rehearsed for the umpteenth time the short path to the holster.

***

Before electing one, Rezo weighed at least five alternative scenarios, each with its pros and cons on how to tackle the security at the intensive care wing. He had a few objectives. First, he wanted the operation non-lethal – after all, the opponents were one of the most fearsome organizations in the world. And for that reason, they were equipped for this mission with traumatic weapons. Second, if there was any emergency button, they needed to act so swiftly as to not give a chance to activate it. For these considerations, Rezo rejected opportunistic options like throwing a tear gas grenade as soon as the elevator doors opened.

Had he made the right choice? He would know in a second. The doors finally opened, and Rezo confidently stepped out and with a broad smile on his face approached the desk, his two accomplices wearing white gowns above their suits following behind. The "greeting committee" was exactly the same as seen on the video.

"Hello, what's going on here? Why are you guarding the entrance?" Rezo was strict, but kept a friendly countenance on his face.

"I ask the questions here." The officer, in his manner, wasn't impressed. "What do you need?"

"I just came all the way from Saint Petersburg on request of the hospital's manager, who said there is a patient here that needs my attention. I'm professor Leibnitz, and with me my assistants."

Maybe the officer was accustomed to professors entering every other second, but none of his facial muscles moved with emotion. He just uttered, "Show your i.d.s."

This was the signal phrase they were all waiting for, meanwhile dispersing to the right positions opposite each of the guards. In unison they reached inside their jackets, produced three guns from the inside, and pointed them into the faces of each of the guards and the officer respectively. Previously rehearsed and done so swiftly, they ensured that none of the guards made a move. Their fingers were still on the AK-47 triggers, but the barrels were kept pointing downwards.

"Easy, boys. I don't want your skulls splattered around here. Keep the guns down, hands up, and move over to the wall." Rezo pointed right.

The first emotion of the day crossed officer's face. It was anger, not subordination or fear. However, at gunpoint he saw no other option but to obey. He slowly stood up, raised his hands, and moved to the wall. The armed guards on both flanks followed suit. They put their Kalashnikovs on the floor and joined their commander.

"Tie them up." Rezo and Akhrik still pointed their guns while Ramaz put zip ties on their hands, tying them behind their backs.

"Frisk them and wait here." Rezo opened the doors and beckoned Ramaz to follow.

Eyeing the third door on the left, Rezo saw only one guard by the door. The less the better, although having another one idle remained at the back of his head.

A nurse headed their way. Losing zero time, Rezo took pepper spray out of another pocket and released it at her face as soon as she came near in such a way that the guard ten meters down the corridor wouldn't notice his move. He just grabbed her from behind and put her gently on the floor as she conked out in a millisecond.

"Help, help!" he yelled, holding her arm as if checking the pulse. The guard reluctantly approached.

"What happened?" He asked and got a stream of gas into his face. In his case, Rezo was less gentle and let him slide down the wall.

All was clear. In a minute or so after leaving the elevator, they had reached the coveted door.

"Stay here," Rezo barked to his subordinate, as he entered the room and appeared nose to nose with someone leaving. In this situ, he let his instincts flow so as not to waste time on thoughts. Rezo took a step back and connected a right hook to the jaw of the guy in front of him. He witnessed shock behind a glimpse of surprise, as the man fell down unconscious. Rezo's fist fighting skills didn't fail.

He saw his prize on the bed opposite the door. "Misha! Rezo!" they exclaimed simultaneously.

Automatically, Rezo registered that Misha's bandages and tubes connected to his body didn't look extremely bad.

"Come, we need to leave fast," Rezo prompted.

Misha tried to stand up, but his one leg faulted and he fell on the floor in pain again.

"Shit." For some reason, Rezo didn't expect this, although he probably should have.

He peeped outside the room and gave a short order. "Get us a wheelchair," he said, meanwhile grabbing Misha off the floor.

The gunshot a second later from the corridor meant that something was wrong.

Chapter 21
Toronto, Canada
<u>Homing in</u>

The reinforcements arrived the next day. Greg was one of the best field operatives, while Yuriy Silvinskiy was an information technology pro, and as side work - a glorious hacker.

Kevin, still under suspected surveillance, met them both in the hotel's lobby, making sure they occupied the most remote and isolated table, and their cellphones were locked in his room. Hopefully, these precautions rendered the chance of eavesdropping to a minimum.

"Ok, guys, we are probably late for a hot pursuit, but we do have here some leads that need to be investigated. I believe you've familiarized yourselves with the brief I sent you, so I won't repeat myself, but if you do have questions – shoot."

"My only question is why you needed me here?" Yuriy, known for his ill-tempered character couldn't resist. "I could check whatever from my office back in London. Internet is equidistant; if anything, I have here fewer options, not more of them."

"I see, but you were summoned here for a reason." Kevin didn't want their mission to start off on the wrong foot and cared to explain. "First, until we've found the leak in our London office, conversing from there is not hermetic. Second, we might need your local support if we find something and attempt to penetrate it. And third, you need to move your fat ass around sometimes; otherwise we'll need to book a double-chair for you even on the first class of an airplane."

Greg grinned; Yuriy burst out laughing. "At least, I hope you have a selection of the best restaurants to supply three meals a day!"

"Don't worry, my friend. If you leave Canada weighing few pounds less, it won't be genocide. Now, back to biz. Greg, take care of the crime scene. Don't think there is much left by local police, but who knows. Yuriy, please try to find some details about this Gertrude -- and of course those bullshit organizations -- and if you could locate someone connected so that Greg and I can meet him or her, that would be fantastic."

"I'll try to." Yuriy finished his coffee and swallowed a pastry, which he had probably managed to order as soon as he entered the hotel.

Greg didn't say anything, but hurried to perform the first task.

***

Greg parked his car at the nearest parking lot and walked towards the adjacent parking place where the woman had been shot. The place was thoroughly cleaned, almost sterilized. The cameras were on, so Greg didn't want to show a lot of suspicious activity; nevertheless, his attentive and trained eye wouldn't miss a thing, if anything was there. Nothing, nothing, and nothing. The police, or "cleaners," had removed all the "interesting" stuff.

He was on the way back when Yuriy called and suggested he check his corporate mailbox, obviously not wanting to speak online.

Greg pulled over, took out his tablet, which was supposed to provide encrypted connection, and entered quickly the corporate cloud. *Hmm. There you go, Ms. Gertrude.* The address was there. Luckily, it was Toronto and not some remote town of this huge country.

Don't put off until tomorrow what you can do today. Someone wise said it, and it perfectly fit Greg's situation. Greg smiled and updated his route for the new address, just entering the consecutive building number, if anyone ever checked his movements in retrospective.

According to the navigation app, the location was off-center, but it didn't take long to get there. Just a few turns once he left the highway. While driving, Greg contemplated the course of action.

Once there, he parked a little further, switched off his phone, and left it in the car, again bearing in mind a subsequent possible triangulation. Not that he intended to harm this Gertrude lady, but precautions were never superfluous.

He walked and finally approached a regular, not very new, but definitely this-century-built edifice. One of those high-rise apartment buildings. No camera was visible by the entrance. *Good, less gadgets to mess with.*

He pressed the apartment "17" button. If someone answered, he wouldn't speak back; he just wanted to see whether someone was home.

The long rings remained unanswered. Undecided whether it was for better or worse, Greg chose to get in.

Picking locks was something Greg could do on the fly. Trying to guess the floor, he pressed six in the elevator and had to go down one flight of stairs to the apartment he was looking for. There were no cameras around. However, the door of apartment eighteen started to open, so Greg retreated quickly one stair up, hoping that whoever had exited hadn't seen him.

After the elevator started its descent carrying the neighbor, Greg returned to the biz. It didn't take more than twenty seconds to pick the lockset with his master. He pried in, hoping there would be no alarm, but was prepared to leave if there was one. Luck was on his side at this point.

With his gloves on, Greg made a quick inspection of the apartment: entrance with adjacent guest bathroom; a spacious living room combined with a kitchen, its island separating two spaces; and one bedroom. She must live here alone, as there were no signs whatsoever of masculine presence: no clothes, shaving tools, or scattered socks.

What caught his attention were two of many notes on a pin board in the kitchen: one was a summons to the police station, which date and time coincided with Greg's intrusion (*Ha!*);   another was a leaflet that read "45°51'26.8"N 78°51'03.4"W," with tomorrow's date and 8.00 P.M. Above the location and date, a smiling man was looking at him from the leaflet with "Paul van Meer" written above the photo. This was unusual. Greg's digital camera grabbed the entire board, just to make sure he didn't miss anything.

He continued the search of the apartment. No computer was visible, but he hoped to find a laptop somewhere. He had just finished with the living area and was about to start on the bedroom when he heard someone at the door.

Chapter 22
Shootout

The shot meant that their operation had suffered an immediate downturn. If Rezo's crewmember had shot someone, he would be here with the wheelchair in a second. Rezo allocated exactly one minute to sit and wait inside Misha's room. However, if his man was shot -- he didn't even want to imagine this scenario, for probably in this case FSB's reinforcements would already be on the way here.

"Akhrik, what's going on?" Rezo used his communication device to contact Akhrik, who had been left by the elevator.

"No idea, something happened inside."

"Ok, stay put."

A minute passed. Everything seemed silent; however, Ramaz didn't show up. Rezo couldn't sit and wait any longer. They needed to leave the hospital as soon as possible.

He opened the door just a crack. There he was. Ramaz's body was ten meters away down the corridor. Seeing no one there except for his man and the still-unconscious nurse, Rezo rushed to his subordinate.

Call it a sixth sense, telepathy, or just training, something told him to turn back. Even before he saw the guard - just at the sight of his shadow -- Rezo started to fall downwards, in time to miss the bullet that hissed very near, as the guard opened fire. Falling backwards, Rezo pulled the trigger, aiming the best he could and shooting in the direction of the guard. Rubber bullets wouldn't kill, but he could hurt and blind the opponent. Years of training paid off again: one of the bullets hit the guard in the face, and he fell down screaming, holding his wound, blood already streaming all over his fingers. Rezo rushed to quiet him with another spray to the face.

Akhrik was still by the ward's door, waiting for his command. "Ramaz is wounded. Come in, find a wheel chair, check how bad it is, and help him. Report back."

Now Misha. Apparently, the entire wing was vacated to isolate him from the outside world. When national security required, other patients could wait or die: no one cared. Opening doors right and left, Rezo saw only empty beds and no patients. In one of the rooms, he spotted a wheelchair and rushed back to Mikhail.

He carefully helped Misha into the chair; put all his tubes, wires and medications across his shoulder; and wheeled him towards the elevator, dodging carefully still-unconscious bodies along the corridor.

"Ramaz is gonna be Ok. Wounded in the right arm and missing the left ear, shot off by a bullet. Unconscious." Alhrik summarized.

Now out, they pressed the elevator's button, making hasty changes back to their civil appearance: two wheelchairs and two standing men -- one suited, the other in a white robe. The doors opened underground and Rezo's heart fell – it was full of people. Some armed.

Instincts and quick hands. The guns were out in milliseconds, barrels pointing towards each other. It was two to four, the balance against Rezo's group. The tension was palpable.

Both groups held their fire, but the tension and a millisecond separating them from the shootout quickly turned unbearable. Luckily, the opponents couldn't know that Rezo's team's weaponry was non-lethal. Nobody exited; no one entered. They stared at each other, ready to shoot, when the elevator's doors started to close.

Rezo's other hand was on the tear gas grenade, and the urge to use it before the doors closed was barely resistible; however, a movement meant bullets, and committing suicide wasn't on his agenda.

The doors didn't reopen. The elevator went up again, which meant getting out of the building necessitated overcoming an armed team waiting below.

Chapter 23
Urgent retreat

Hide, retreat, confront. These were Greg's options. The key was turning. The job was done; he didn't need complications. He rushed to the balcony. If retreat was impossible, he would need to confront whoever entered the place. The window curtain blocked the view of the balcony from the inside. However, it could be moved aside any second. Glancing up and down, Greg to his awe didn't see a safe way to get out. He flung himself closer to the door to try to hear who was inside. He heard multiple voices: ". . . to the kitchen. Check every drawer. The lonely ladies sometimes make it their favorite place. I'll take a look in the bedroom. Hey, Jim, how about you start from here?"
Shit. It sounded like police with a search warrant. The least pleasant encounter, in Greg's book. This reduced options to two: hide or run. There was nowhere to hide on the balcony. He could sit behind the griller or even pack himself underneath it, but diligent cops (and he needed to assume they were) would get there sooner or later.
He looked outside again. The balconies went diagonally. The one underneath was two floors down. By jumping down there, he risked breaking a leg or, if not, a neck. Sideways, there were balconies on the left and right side

just a floor down, but at some distance. The right one was crammed with stuff, so Greg chose to go for the left one.

He climbed the balcony's outer barrier, holding the wall with one hand for balance. *Holy shit.* The distance was risky, maybe out of reach.

Before he could lose courage, evaluating the distance, the possible fall and all other jeopardies, Greg just made his best leap forward trying to put into it as much strength and thrust as he could. The impact was inevitable: he hit the rail with his torso, caught it with his hands, and rolled in onto the balcony's floor. *Damn that hurt.* Greg was sure that he had fractured or broken a rib or two.

Now what? Moaning from pain, his stream of thoughts was interrupted by a woman's shriek, and someone rushed towards him from inside the apartment.

"What happened? Are you hurt? I'll call an ambulance. How did you get here? What happened? Are you hurt?" The woman seemed utterly shocked and unable to stop shooting questions.

"Ma'am, help. My ribs are broken. I jumped off the balcony above."

"From Peterson's? Oh, my god. That's two floors. Oh, my God. Why would you do that? I need to call Sam. Are you local?"

That she assumed he had jumped from Peterson's apartment was even better. "No, ma'am. I'm their guest from London. I lost my key and needed to get out. So silly of me jumping down like that. I could've easily died here." Greg with his

Cockney couldn't possibly pass for a Canadian. He was coming to his senses much sooner than his host.

"Please, ma'am, show me where to get out. I need to take myself to the hospital. Please, thank you." Greg managed to get up, his face distorted from pain.

"I'll call the ambulance. You can't go by yourself. Wait."

"No, no, no, it's Ok. I gotta go. Please."

The panicky woman ushered him to the door "Are you sure? Are you Ok? Oh, my."

"Thank you, thank you." Greg hurried.

Maybe it was his imagination, but he could swear he heard her saying, "The world must've gone totally nuts, if people start falling from the sky in broad daylight onto my balcony. Totally crazy."

Greg grinned through pain from his poor impromptu performance that had actually worked, and pressed the elevator button. After jumping one floor down, he chose the comfort of the elevator to descend to the ground.

The mysterious rendezvous with Paul van Meer sat on his mind. After checking, with Yuriy's help, some initial info on this figure and discovering that some intelligence reports tagged him as "the leader of various Marxist and extreme left-oriented organizations" both over- and underground, their common confidence that they needed to meet him grew. Some of the intel mentioned "trained security detail."

Chapter 24
Escape

Where the hell did they come from? Rezo couldn't believe this unlucky coincidence. They just needed a few more minutes to escape. There was no time for grievance, and Rezo understood it.

"Bijo, bring the car alongside the building. Look where you can come close to the wall; we'll be leaving through the window. Fast. Take into account that there are at least four FSB down in the building. Maybe more. In the meantime, send Givi to the hall to see if maybe he can surprise them from the outside with a tear gas grenade or lock them up or anything. Copy." He communicated to the driver left in the car.

"Ok, sir. We are on it."

Back at the empty ward, Rezo rushed to the window to watch out for their minivan. With two disabled people on his hands, his fighting options were very limited.

"Akhrik, take sheets and blankets, tie them up together. We need a rope to get down to the ground. Hurry." *Who said movie tricks couldn't work?*

The minibus made its way around the building, left the road, and headed straight across the lawn, leaving an ugly two-line trajectory in neatly-kept grass and flowerbeds that separated the building from the hospital's internal roads. It stopped right beneath the window, from which Rezo was waving.

Rezo heard an explosion below and felt a slight tremor of its echo. Must've been Givi engaging the team below somehow. *Just don't get anyone killed,* Rezo thought, but didn't voice it on the radio.

"The elevator's going up!" someone yelled on the communication line.

"Jam the doors. Cut the power, disable it somehow and retreat." Rezo barked back.

The improvised rope was ready.

"The wounded first." Misha more ordered than suggested and pointed at the wounded combatant.

"Alright." Rezo didn't have time for arguing.

They tied a rope around his body and lowered him to Bijo's waiting hands on the ground. The passers-by started to crowd, and some approached to see what was going on or to offer help.

Bijo took his comrade to the car and, lacking inventiveness, just roared at those who volunteered to help, "Go away! It's under control."

Misha was next. His hands were too weak to hold the rope, so he was bundled and lowered the same way as the fighter before him.

"Now, quick." They fixed the rope to a metal bed, which in its turn was fixed to the wall and descended one after another.

Akhrik, going last, couldn't make it at first, as someone tried to pull him back up, so he had to jump from the third-floor height, while Rezo opened fire aiming near the window to keep the adversaries back inside the room. Akhrik tried to regroup and cushion the landing, but his shriek while rolling on the ground meant that he had probably broken one or both of his legs.

"Oh, my, I'm gonna end this mission with everyone crippled," Rezo couldn't help commenting.

He, Bijo, and Givi, who joined them running away from the entrance -- the only ones still standing -- raised their guns in unison and shot at the window where the camouflaged FSB team had reappeared. They backed away.

"Let's get outta here." They hadn't gotten far enough when the bullets hit the minibus's roof. A few made it through, and it was sheer luck that no one else was wounded or killed.

The sound of the siren meant the pursuit was on. They were in the middle of Russia, kilometers from the border. Tooth and nail wouldn't suffice. They needed something extra.

"Keep going, baby. Try to lose them." Rezo gave orders, simultaneously rethinking the escape route.

They had a minivan on their tail with tinted windows and two barrels on both sides ready to spray Rezo and his crew. The pursuers would multiply momentarily, as probably the police and FSB radio waves were red hot with reports and alarms.

Ultimately, they needed to get to the airport; however, Rezo began to understand that it wouldn't work. The airport would be the first place where FSB would look for them, even if they lost their tail now.

He didn't have time to think it all through, so he relied on instinct more than on planning. Soon they'd need to get rid of the phones to become untraceable. A moment before doing that, he dialed David.

"The situ is tight, we have Misha, but everybody in this country will soon be after us. Abort pick up at Pashkovsky airport. Instead have three different planes ready in Sochi for tomorrow. We'll all be offline soon. I'll let you know as soon as I can."

"I count on you, Rezo. Good luck. How's Misha?"

"Not in his best shape, but holding well. If we get out, he's gonna be Ok. Sorry, Dave, need to switch back to biz." He hung up. The immediate plan was to replace this vehicle with two others that had been prepared in advance, and disperse.

Chapter 25
Forest abduction
(*The chapter is written by Graeme Rodaughan*)

Moonlight speared through the great boles of the forest, dappling the forest floor in pale splotches.

Kevin followed the GPS on his cellphone, thankful it was still operational this far out into the forest. He strode along a fire trail wide enough to support vehicle access, Yuriy and Greg following closely behind him. The trail sloped gently upward; they were heading for a low hilltop. A noted tourist spot, but currently deserted due to public works. It was at the exact location that matched the GPS coordinates found by Greg in Ms. Gertrude's Toronto apartment.

He checked the map once again. They were less than a thousand meters from the site. He put his cellphone away. It was time to maximize stealth as they approached the site of Paul van Meer's address to his followers. He glanced over his shoulder at Greg and Yuriy, trailing a couple of meters behind him. Greg was looking grim from the long walk. He'd broken his ribs the day before and soldiered on with a massive amount of taping around his ribcage and a steady supply of painkillers. Kevin pressed his lips into a thin line. His best fighter was limited by his injuries. He'd have to plan around Greg's reduced capability to achieve mission success.

What was the mission? Abduct van Meer. It sounded good on paper, but achieving it was another matter. They'd parked the car a kilometer back from the site and walked up the trail. They'd left the car facing back down the trail to enable a quick getaway – if they got back to it in one piece. The GPS map on his cellphone had indicated that the trail looped through the site – there was only one way in and one way out. If he was in charge of Paul's security, he'd have a close watch on the approach to the site.

A gleam of golden light flickered ahead of them. Kevin halted for a moment, breathing quietly, standing as still as a statue. The light continued to dance, faint crowd noises filtering through the night air. He chopped his hand to the right and led his small team off the trail and into the woods.

Kevin thanked the full moon and star-filled sky. Conditions were perfect for a slow, stealthy approach through the woods. He led Greg and Yuriy from tree to tree, scanning the woods ahead of him before every step. It took time to approach the site this way, but being discovered and captured were not options he cared to contemplate. There was no doubt that van Meer's thugs would leave their bloodied and broken bodies in nearby shallow graves if they got their hands on Kevin and his teammates.

He finally approached close enough to see a broad clearing lit by four large bonfires. Kevin crouched behind a fallen tree trunk. Greg and Yuriy took up positions to the left and right, peering over the forest giant at the clearing. A broad circular area stood before them. It was easily two-hundred meters across. Four bonfires blazed on the inside edges of the clearing perimeter. On the northern edge of the clearing, farthest from the trail entrance, van Meer stood in the back of a dark-blue Ford one-tonne truck. The truck was lit with a number of lights creating a stage. Paul held a megaphone and addressed the crowd.

Kevin didn't focus on the words. He wasn't here to listen to one of van Meer's speeches. He scanned the site. There were a pair of guards about fifty meters to their right facing out into the woods, armed with submachine guns. Beyond them and to the right of Paul's stage were three black Chevy Suburbans.

Greg whispered, "There's six security staff in front of the stage, and I think I can make out another two on the far side of the clearing."

Yuriy faced right and squinted. "There's another pair of guards past the Ford pickup truck."

Kevin summed up, "Okay, we've got six guards in front of the truck. Three pairs of guards are facing out into the woods to the north, west and east." He paused for a moment scanning to the south along the trail. His eyes narrowed with recognition. "And another two at the trail mouth for a total of fourteen guys all armed with submachine guns."

"We can't take these bastards on," Yuriy hissed. "They've got way too much firepower!"

Kevin grinned wryly. "I'm not planning on a frontal assault." He stared hard at the Ford pickup truck. Electrical leads ran from beneath the hood to the lights shining on van

Meer and his impromptu stage. Every now and then, van Meer would pause; the crowd would hush; and the low rumble of an idling V8 would drift across the clearing. He turned to Yuriy and asserted, "Yuriy, my good friend – I need you to be bait."

"What?" Yuriy said, his eyes widening and his face blanching beneath the moonlight.

***

It was a crazy plan and Yuriy was certain he was an idiot for agreeing to do it, but what the hell – Kevin was the boss. Yuriy sidled around the back of the rearmost Chevy SUV and strolled as nonchalantly as he could manage toward the front of the line of three vehicles. There were a pair of heavies armed with submachine guns on guard duty twenty meters past the lead vehicle. By some miracle they didn't see him until he reached the last SUV.

The closest thug flung his hand out at him and shouted, "Hey, You! Get away from there."

Yuriy ripped the zipper down on the front of his pants, fumbled for half a second getting his cock out, then began pissing on the front wheel of the Chevy Suburban. He leaned back with a loud sigh, waving his stream of piss left and right over the wheel. He leered at the approaching guard in what he hoped was a drunken manner and slurred cheerily, "Up the workers!"

"Fuck!" exclaimed the other guard. "Sergei, get this drunken prick back into the crowd."

The nearer bruiser, undoubtedly Sergei, was almost upon him. Yuriy lifted his hands, still peeing, and pleaded, "I can't stop now."

"I don't care," Sergei snarled. He stepped forward to slap a heavy hand on Yuriy's shoulder. Yuriy turned to face him; his stream of urine slashing across the guard's neatly-pressed trousers and showering his buffed leather shoes.

The guard leaped back in disgust, his face darkening underneath the moonlight and the glow of the floodlights on the Ford pickup truck.

The crowd roared with laughter at something van Meer said. The other guard was down on the ground. Kevin and Greg had done a number on him and were stepping away from his limp body.

Sergei growled, strode forward, and swung a fist like a sledge hammer at Yuriy's face. Yuriy whirled away. The fist sailed past the back of his head as he stumbled forward away from the guard. He slid awkwardly on the gravel of the track and nearly lost his balance completely. He recovered and turned around. Sergei was already down, unconscious and propped up by Kevin and Greg against the side of the SUV.

Greg winced, held his ribs with both hands, and whispered hoarsely, "Shit that hurt."

"Not as much as it's going to hurt when they wake up," Kevin asserted, flipping a sharp knife out of his pocket. He swung his hand down fast and stabbed the blade deep into the nearest tire. The air escaped in a rush and the SUV leaned over a few centimeters. He repeated the operation another five times, disabling all the wheels on the forest side of the line of SUVs.

He returned to Greg and Yuriy and sheathed his knife. "Okay," he directed, lifting Sergei's submachine gun and glancing across the hood of the SUV at the back of van Meer standing in the tray of the pickup truck. "You two get into the Ford's cabin and take off. I'll be on the back with van Meer."

Yuriy zipped up his pants and glanced at Greg. It was a certainty that the other guards wouldn't be standing around with their thumbs up their butts while they rolled out of here with their boss.

Kevin slapped him on the back. "Go!"

Yuriy ran after Greg for the front of the Ford pickup truck.

***

Kevin followed his men toward the Ford pickup truck. Van Meer shouted something about eating the rich, and the crowd cheered. Greg pulled the right-hand side door of the truck's cabin open and leaped inside. Yuriy scrambled in after him. The pickup was left-hand drive; Greg would be seizing the steering wheel in seconds.

Kevin had to be quick or he'd be left behind. He reached for the rim of the tray and launched himself into the back of the

107

pickup truck. He spun as he landed, his left leg sweeping van Meer's feet out from under him. Van Meer collapsed with a startled yelp. Kevin flipped over and drove the back of van Meer's skull into the steel floor of the tray -- hard enough to knock him unconscious, but artfully judged not to kill him.

He needed him alive. Van Meer's security team started yelling and shouting. They were at most twenty meters away from the other side of the truck. They'd be onto them in seconds. Kevin pulled his knife with his free hand and shouted, "Go! Go! Go!"

The Ford's engine howled as Greg planted his foot on the accelerator. The pickup truck lurched forward. The floodlights fell away to the left, snapping into darkness, leaving only the bonfires to light the clearing.

The half dozen closest guards rushed the truck. One made it to the rim of the tray and grabbed hold, swinging himself up.

Kevin stabbed the guard's hand with his knife. Blood splashed, and the man yelled, "Fuck," as he lost his grip and fell away.

The Ford's wheels spun on the gravel, the truck swerving out onto the track. Kevin risked a quick glance above the rim of the tray. The six guards in front of the impromptu stage were down to five, with one cradling his bleeding hand. They were sprinting across the clearing to intercept the accelerating Ford.

Kevin flicked his head right. Another two guards outside the circle of the track were lining their guns up on the

Ford's tires. *Damn it. If they shot out the tires, the truck would slow and the rest of the guards would swamp them.* The pickup truck lurched as it straddled a set of potholes. The track was more of a goat path than a superhighway.

He straight-armed his submachine gun and fired a short burst in the two guards' general direction. They dived aside as the bullets slashed over their heads, striking bark off the trees behind them.

On Kevin's front-left flank, one of the four bonfires loomed. Greg smashed the truck through its gears. The engine howled as the Ford raced forward. The five guards sprinting across the clearing veered to their left in an attempt to catch up with the Ford. The pickup truck raced past the bonfire, positioning the roaring flames between the guards and the fleeing truck.

They baulked, spreading to the left and right. The two nearest guards opened fire upon the truck, bullets stitching their way along the flank of the vehicle. Someone shouted behind them, "Stop firing! You'll hit the boss."

Kevin had banked on the guards not firing at him as they accelerated away, for fear of hitting van Meer. He hadn't taken account of the crowd. They'd scattered at the sound of gun fire; twenty or more were running across the trail in front of the truck.

Greg slammed the horn and downshifted the gears. The engine roared like a lion on steroids, and the crowd scattered off the track, diving left and right as the Ford pickup barreled along the gravel pathway circling the clearing. They passed the last bonfire on the right, again using it as cover from the five pursuing security guards.

Kevin risked a last glance back. The guards were hopelessly enmeshed within the panicked crowd. He breathed a sigh of relief and then looked forward. The last two guards at the entrance to the clearing, at the throat of the road back out of the forest, were sighting down their weapons at the front of the truck.

There was no evidence that the stock-standard Ford was armored or had bulletproof glass. The two guards could fill the cabin with lead, slaughtering Greg and Yuriy in an instant. Kevin twisted up, flinging his right arm over the top of the cabin. He pulled hard on the submachine gun's trigger, firing a long burst at the two men.

The first lifted back, a row of bullet holes appearing across his chest as he fell back in a pink mist of his own blood. The second guard fired back, sparks flying away from the front of the Ford. Glass smashed as rounds hammered into the cabin.

Kevin swung his gun left, brass casings flying into the night. The last guard lurched backward and fell away with a hoarse yell. The Ford rushed forward, swerved to the right around the last guard's position, and shot off down the road and away from the clearing.

Kevin looked back; there was no one following – yet. He pounded on the top of the cabin with his fist and yelled, "Are you okay in there?"

"Fuck, yeah," Greg shouted back.

"I'm okay," Yuriy called out.

Kevin turned and checked van Meer. He was unhurt, just unconscious, breathing well with a steady pulse. Kevin pulled a plastic zip tie from his pocket and bound van Meer's wrists. Satisfied that their high-value prisoner wasn't going anywhere, he looked back at the cabin.

There were a pair of bullet holes in the glass panel at the back of the cabin. The 9mm slugs must've passed between his legs when he was exchanging fire with the last two guards.

A loud bang erupted from the engine, and it started blowing steam and smoke. The Ford lurched. They'd covered half a kilometer and were still going downhill. They only needed to make another half kilometer to reach their car. They'd leave the truck parked across the road, locked up with the park brake on. Just another obstacle to slow down any pursuit.

The Ford continued to run, churning out plumes of oily smoke and pale steam, chasing the twin cones of its headlights into the night. The trees whipped past, disappearing into the gloom behind them. Kevin sat down behind the cabin and regarded van Meer.

In another couple of minutes, they would transfer to their own car and get the hell out of the forest. No one could stop them from doing that. Kevin had van Meer right where he wanted him. He pursed his lips. There was only one question left - could he keep him?

He'd mounted the tiger; now all he had to do was ride it.

Chapter 26
Exit

I tried not to interfere and bombard Rezo and his men with questions. Barely escaping from the hospital and being chased by FSB and -- undoubtedly, soon -- by police, I relied on him to do the job, like I always had on Arthur when he was around.

The streets were relatively empty for this late evening hour, but we managed to keep our distance and didn't let them get near enough for shooting. Each screech of tires and sharp maneuver caused me pain, but it was something I was accustomed to lately. Our advantage over the pursuers might not last forever, and we could expect road blocks to be prepared ahead.

"Wipe and leave all your phones on the floor." Rezo seemed cool and in control of the situ. "We switch cars two blocks from here. Misha comes with me. Givi, you take Ramaz with you. Forget about the airport. Try to get out of town soonest. We meet tomorrow at Adler near Sochi's airport at 1300 sharp."

The driver, who didn't look familiar, took a sharp right, then another one, and then left. A hundred meters down the narrow street he turned into the arch under a shabby building and went to the left of the spacious inner yard.

Well prepared. I hoped those behind us weren't near enough to trace our trajectory. The driver parked near two cars that appeared to be waiting for our arrival. A metallic sedan and Russian Niva jeep.

"Come, Misha, put your arm around my neck." Rezo easily and gently grabbed me off the chair and placed me on the back seat of the jeep. "Fasten your seat belt, Sir. Gotta hit fishermen woodways soon."

I tried to relax, but with guns and bullets pointed at me during the last few days way too often, it wasn't easy.

"Givi, go first. Report if all is clear out the gate. After we split, turn communications off. Turn them back on when reaching Adler tomorrow."

Givi probably okayed our exit, as our car commenced its movement a few seconds after Givi's. This time Rezo took the wheel.

"Good preparations, Rezo." I couldn't help sharing my sigh of relief.

"Thanks. Too early to cheer, though. They'll cordon off all major highways, airports, train stations, and we'll need to think hard how to hoodwink them in order to leave Russia unnoticed. The sooner we do it the better, because the more time the authorities have, the tighter will the pressure around us become."

"So, what's the plan?" We were still cruising about Krasnodar.

"An immediate one is to escape this town and then try to cover distance on dirt roads. At first glance, we can pass for a believable fishing or hunting company. Don't you think?"

Niva was one of the most popular vehicles for exactly this purpose.

"Yeah, fishing or hunting sounds like another life at the moment, especially when everyone's hunting you." I couldn't help being a bit acrimonious.

Rezo tried to find an exit from the city via secondary roads. The further we went, the shabbier the districts looked; we were entering some semi-deserted industrial zone. Manufacturing seemed to have abandoned these once busy and boisterous places. What could I expect? From an industrial giant, former USSR had turned into mostly a consumer economy: import stuff from China and sell it to local dudes; export limitless raw materials to somewhere where manufacturing still worked. Producing something on its own entailed too much hassle and couldn't compete with cheap Chinese merchandise. The businessman and politician in me started to wake.

The industrial zone ended, leaving us on the reinforced concrete plates forming a road going alongside the railway.

I hoped stage one was accomplished and we had managed to escape the city smoothly.

However, the smooth beginning of the trip could mean a rough ending, as I found out rather quickly.

Chapter 27
Hearty welcome

"Oh, comrade Paul, so nice to see you." Torn with anxiety on the inside, David was beaming with sarcasm and false hospitality on the outside. "How was your trip, comfy? Surprised to be elevated straight into the lion's den?"

Paul van Meer had just been thrust into David's office, still tied, gagged, and apparently simmering.

"Good job, Kevin, after all," David praised. "Come, join me in our little chat with the dearest guest that condescended to accept our warm invitation."

"You're starting to sound like Mikhail," Kevin grinned.

"Yeah, do I? Well, spending too many years with him since our student time must've left a malign impact on my personality." Hearing that Misha was with friends, although still in danger, nonetheless made him feel joyful.

David didn't like the nasty style anyway. He approached their prisoner, tore off the tape over his mouth, and took the gag out.

Now the rage became more evident: van Meer breathed heavily and darted his gazes like lightning strikes.

"Come, grab a seat, you can't kill me, darling. At least not just yet, so we might as well be pleasant to each other. A drink, a cigar?" David, wearing a navy suit, squared shirt and tie, played the perfect English gentleman. It would look comical, if it wasn't dead serious.

"You'll regret…"

"Yeah, yeah, I've heard that so many times," David interrupted him outright. "You might as well rethink your strategy, because if anything bad befalls us, you'll need to work hard to survive. I have moods and my good mood can disappear like a hot and sunny day can abruptly change into a downpour." David still felt poetic.

The captive Marxist leader fell silent, as if indeed contemplating his further reaction. Smart guy, he grabbed a glass, poured himself a half of single malt scotch and drank it all up in a few gulps.

"Impressive drinking techniques, pal." David, who would drink the same quantity much slower, was truly impressed.

"I can't save your boss," the "neo- Lenin" switched to business mode.

"Thank you very much, no need. He's on the way to greet you personally, I hope."

Van Meer looked genuinely surprised.

"What, you don't believe me? The FSB snatched him out of the hands of your Russian goons."

Paul underwent a sudden transformation and began laughing wholeheartedly.

Befuddled, David couldn't quite understand his reaction. "What's so funny?"

"FSB is one of our sponsors," he tried to compose himself.

"Shit, really? So, what was it: just a change of decorations?"

"Exactly!"

Snatching him out had been the right move. David praised himself and hoped Misha was out of their reach for good.

Chapter 28
The lull before the storm

Finally seated by the campfire, we could relax and talk without the need to address the pressing reality every minute. In the high fishing season, bonfires were scattered across the entire country, so ours shouldn't attract any attention whatsoever.

I took Rezo to the side, as his subordinates were new to me, and I couldn't confide in them like I did in Rezo. We had a long record of friendship, money made together, and quite a few personal experiences.

I knew he respected me, maybe even adored, and responded in kind. You don't miss out on people like this crossing your lifepath.

"Appreciate you risking your life for me, friend." I felt an urge to thank him.

"Ah, no worries – we share the same code of not leaving friends in trouble." Rezo dismissed my gratitude, probably feeling uneasy with these soul talks.

"True, however I never take it for granted. Hope we can get out of Russia. Becomes kinda toxic here."

"Yep, the pressure is in the air; we both know that as we speak, they put more and more efforts in locating us and tightening up the country to prevent our escape."

"So, what's our plan? I imagine it shouldn't be just a pure improvisation?"

"Well, the original plan was busted by this unlucky encounter at the elevator and ensuing pursuit, so now – it's indeed more of an improvisation. We need to get to the airport farther out of Krasnodar, hope that the planes are there, and get you through the authorities, assuming they'll be on the lookout. I have an idea or two to toy with." Rezo was anything but complacent, despite the relaxing warmth of the fire and refreshing aroma of coniferous forest. Maybe I was the boss; however, he was at the helm of this rescue operation. "In general, we'll try to smuggle you in for a supposedly domestic flight, but once airborne – the sky is literally the limit. How's your leg doing … err, what's left of it?"

"Don't ask, you can't even imagine how it is to feel like a cripple and to be so dependent. Just a burden in this race. On the other hand, allowing for where I was just a few days ago, even survival is not trivial, so I guess I shouldn't complain. It's in those moments when you look into the eyes of death, you make those silly resolutions and hope your life is spared for a reason. However, it's early to celebrate yet. Let's see what happens tomorrow." The lull of the night out in the wilderness contributed to the philosophical and confessional mood. Or maybe it was the chacha – a Georgian grape vodka that Rezo poured me.

I added wood to the bonfire, whose flames had died down lower than they should to my liking. Business and world matters left so little room for these simple pleasures. I reminisced nostalgically about my childhood, when making a bonfire was almost a weekly thing. Another flash of memory came: Masha and that special romantic evening we had what felt like light years ago on the beach of the Kiev sea. The feelings then were still fresh and strong and maybe our daughter was conceived that evening. At least the dates supported that theory, when we tried to trace it back. I regretted that life took us so much apart and missed those moments when there was passion, care, respect, when we were one piece. If someone was to be blamed, it would be me, mostly.

Yeah, it's definitely chacha. I felt like dozing off. This fifty-percent strong beverage took control of me.

"Rezo, I'm gonna take a nap." I used a tall branch that one of Rezo's guys had cut for me as a cane and moved towards my sleeping bag.

Despite all the anxieties, troubles, anticipations, and everything this wicked world had in store for me to cope with, I fell asleep almost instantaneously, and Rezo's prompting me to wake up at sunrise felt only moments away from the previous night.

Ok, then, we've got some business to handle. I felt prepared for the new challenge of this fateful day.

Chapter 29
Airport

Yeah, a Russian jeep was supposed to be able to cope with Russian roads. But barely so – the ride resembled taming a mustang. Starting our journey at 06:30, it took us five hours to leave a sufficient distance behind, before Rezo risked returning to the highway. From there it was quicker. We reached the vicinity of the airport by the afternoon, and Rezo switched the communication on again to check where the other car was.

They were near! They reported changing drivers along the way, never stopping until they were close enough. They then parked in a remote position near a gasoline station and waited for our arrival.

So far, we had somehow managed to avoid roadblocks. Despite whatever forged documents we had, whatever explanations and masquerade we could offer, we were sure that any crippled person on the road in the given circumstances would be thoroughly checked before being cleared.

My photograph and biometric data had probably been circulated as well.

After a short consultation with Givi and two more of his subordinates, Rezo made up his mind and started instructing the teams.

"Alico, Bijo and Davit," Rezo looked at each of them – most of the "still standing, "go with Givi. You drive straight to the airport and wait for my command to approach the VIP desk for private jets. You're gonna pass it first and report back info on the security arrangements. We might need some commotion there."

"Akhrik, Ramaz, you come with me and Mikhail. We'll need a short detour into Sochi."

Everyone dispersed between the two cars, while Rezo helped me limp towards the Lada. Ramaz, with a wounded and bandaged arm, functioned normally; only an occasional grimace reflected the pain.

Rezo pulled over at the first big computer store, told me to wait in the car, and soon returned with a tablet, two SIM cards, and a functional new cell phone. He quickly set up a new Skype account, phoned our secret corporate hotline, and asked them to pass to David a message to urgently connect with the Russian number of the anonymous phone that he'd just purchased.

Multiple precautions couldn't guarantee privacy, but maybe they could buy us some time, before those who monitored communication on the Russian side would be able to put two and two together and connect it to us.

Soon we heard an unrecognizable voice, but the code word "malina" (raspberry) meant it was David. Seasoned by battles and conflicts, a sizeable wing of our corporate research department worked on advanced stuff to hoodwink voice identifiers and developed other gadgetry for sale and for internal use as well. One of our inventions that was being tested, pre-patent stage, was a voice distorter, as we assumed voice recognition filters were helping intelligence agencies to sift through the tsunami of voice traffic. They had demonstrated an operational model to me six months ago, but still I was amused at how deeply it changed the voice that I had heard by my side almost daily since I was a student.

"Are you there?" David, sounding not David, addressed me.

"He's here, no worries," Rezo replied instead. "But we don't have the same gadget on this side to put him online."

They both avoided referencing me by my name.

"I understand. Well, good luck there, guys. Everything that you've asked for is in place."

"Are the drivers ours or chartered?" Rezo called pilots "drivers" just in case certain words were specifically monitored, as I understood.

"Ours, of course, the best people. Won't hesitate to drive you anywhere," David got the drift.

"Thanks, gotta go, tell them to warm up."

"Good luck!" Even distorted, David's voice conveyed concern.

***

The communication procurement detour took less than an hour. The half of Rezo's men who had gone straight to the airport were supposed to be there, hopefully after passing through all the formalities.

We were near the gate leading to the airfield when the communication device crackled and we heard, "Run! They got us. They'll be..." Givi was interrupted and then we heard a *kkhh,* as if someone had busted the mike by stepping on it.

The same second, a few camouflaged fighters ran out of the guard booth by the gate with their barrels aimed at our car and scattered, forming a semicircle.

"Lay down!" Rezo yelled to me.

I didn't know what he was thinking about, but he accelerated and went speeding straight into the gate.

Hissing bullets punctured the hull of the car, an impact from hitting the gate, all that mixed together as one scary moment. The car kept going, so I dared to raise my head just a little to look back.

One person was lying on the ground, maybe hit by a car. Others... four, no... five were chasing us on foot and shooting their Kalachs at the same time.

"Is anyone hurt?" Rezo yelled, as we heard a low moan.

"I, it's Okay." Ramaz, sitting near him, was holding this time his bleeding shoulder.

We were on the airfield, making distance between ourselves and our pursuers. Rezo zigzagged a bit until we were far enough that the shooting stopped. He went straight to the private jets parking. Sochi was full of them -- there were maybe more of them than of commercial airliners, since it was a "compulsory" resort, prescribed by the authorities out of fake patriotism for the most Russian elite businessmen and politicians, which resulted in a steady influx of superrich locals and their superrich peers from abroad.

"What about Givi and the others?" I couldn't help asking, feeling guilty that they had been apprehended because of me. "We don't leave our men behind."

"Getting them now would be suicide. We must get you out of here first." Rezo didn't budge.

The pilot of one of the planes stepped out onto the stairs, waving to us. I recognized him. Bud or Greg or something short, whose services we had used years ago when smuggling armaments to our friends in Africa.

"Welcome aboard, Sir!" He greeted me with a broad smile.

"Err… the authorities are after us, they won't let you take off." I returned him a firm handshake, while leaning on the car.

His smile became even broader, "Hurry then." It always surprised me how the world would never run out of this type of cutthroat adventurer that just embraced the challenge, whether from bravery or stupidity.

Rezo returned to commanding. "Disperse between the planes. We need them uncertain as to which plane Misha embarked. Move it. I'll carry each of you, play it injured."

I didn't understand at first what for, but then it dawned on me that the airport was full of cameras, so he wanted to show "disabled" passengers on each plane.

Rezo stayed on the same plane with me. Akhrik and now twice-wounded Ramaz boarded the other two – one in each.

"We go second," Rezo told the pilot. The neighboring plane taxied from the parking spot, with us and the other plane right behind him.

"Hurry!" We all heard sirens.

Bud, now I was sure of his name, switched the engines on to warm up. It seemed the airport had announced a closure, since no planes were landing or taking off, and at least two were circling above, waiting for permission to land.

Warily, I looked out the window in all directions, trying to spot military planes and anti-air missiles, with WW2 air fights movies in my head. Except now it wasn't a movie: I was to star in a reality show. Mostly Boeings and Airbuses with an occasional Ilyushin or Tupolev were scattered among the parking zones, as far as my sight reached, but who could vouch that there was nothing else?

"Oh, crap, they've blocked the runway!" Rezo had just realized that and drew pilot's attention.

"Shit, this will be risky, but we can try. Dennis, use lane five for takeoff!"

I looked out the window to check where it was. *Mama mia!* It was just a secondary route between the parking areas – maybe long enough but hardly prepared for takeoffs. I hoped they had enough experience from impromptu airfields in Africa to pull it off.

Maybe those pilots didn't think it was that crazy an idea, as I saw the first plane turning left and speeding up. If they could do it, we could too.

I recalled a scandal with a German boy landing some semi-amateur aircraft on the Red Square after passing through all the mighty defenses and radars not long before the Big Bang of the USSR. *Can we make it?*

***

We couldn't wait until the air stabilized after the takeoff of the first plane. Bud started speeding even before Dennis was airborne.

I saw pieces of the ground torn away and jumping up along our route. Damn, they were shooting! I started to pray. The runway all of a sudden became too long to bear. *Bud, get away, please!* My heart was pounding and adrenaline pumped through the system, cold sweat running down my forehead. Probably never before had I wanted to leave Russia and stay alive as badly as I wanted it that moment.

And then we were airborne! The plane commenced conquering altitude in what felt like the maximum angle of attack. This Bud was an ace!

I looked back. The third plane had made it into the air too! Thank God!

My joy quickly turned into awe and I gasped for air, acute pain paralyzing me, when I noticed that the third plane's left engine was on fire, and it was taking a critical dive down.

"They were hit!" I yelled, unable to control myself.

Rezo saw it too. We tracked the falling plane until it hit the surface of the Black Sea, jumped and dived back into the waves, parts falling off it with each collision, then disappearing into the depths, remnants floating, scattered around.

Rezo crossed himself, murmuring something about salvation of souls.

I heard Bud from the cabin. "Den, go West, I go South. Let them figure which one they need. Stick to other planes en route in hope they won't dare shoot and endanger them." The voice was firm, business-like. Obviously, he couldn't be distracted for grieving even for a millisec lest we repeated the same fate.

I didn't hear the response; however, our plane tilted left, flying southbound. I couldn't help counting, hoping we could cover enough distance before some MiGs or Sukhoys were scrambled, or they started shooting their fearsome antiair arsenal.

611, 612, 613. I wiped my forehead and dared another gaze out. Clouds were separating us from the ground, creating an illusion of peaceful and sunny surroundings. At first, I didn't understand what it was, as two projectiles tore through the clouds at some distance but not very far away and went up and above. *Fucking rockets!*

This nightmare was about to end one way or another.

I took out a cellphone that Rezo had just bought and given me, added my wife's number to the memory. It was one of the very few that I remembered by heart anyway, and I wrote a WhatsApp message -- *Masha, love you and kids* -- and pressed "Send."

The phone was offline, of course, but if it were ever recovered, I wanted these to be my last words.

We either hit some severe turbulence or that was how Bud tried to avoid the missiles, but the plane was rocking from insane maneuvers, gaining and losing altitude almost every second and tilting left and right.

Two more rockets hit the cloud behind us. Much closer this time. Den's plane wasn't visible anymore.

845, 846... I still counted, my palms gripping the arms of the chair in a desperate longing for some stability. Unable to take it any longer, I unbuckled and tried to reach the minibar, but fell and rolled, guided by another abrupt maneuver.

"Misha, sit still, please, do me a favor." Rezo had to leap out of his chair to help me.

"Hold on, guys!" Bud shouted from the cabin, after hearing what to him must've sounded like a skirmish.

"Rezo, mate, can you get me something from the minibar?" I felt on the verge of panic and hoped alcohol would calm me down.

We were in a sharp nosedive and the sea looked on a rapid approach. Bud returned the plane into a horizontal flight at the clouds level.

"I see planes on the radar. We need to last a few more minutes, and hopefully they'll stop firing." This time Bud used the loudspeaker.

The plane stabilized, and Rezo reached for the fridge, took a bottle of scotch, made sure I was ready, and tossed it to me. I unscrewed it and took a long gulp. Dying drunk didn't sound like the worst sin to me.

The plane started to climb, while taking a sharp right. About twenty minutes must've passed since takeoff, and we were still in the air. If they stopped firing, I hoped sending military planes to intercept us would be too much even for Russia, but possibly I underestimated their resolve.

A short lull in air acrobatics allowed me to resume counting. After five more minutes, measured by counting three hundred more, I took another long gulp.

I was afraid to believe it, but it looked like we'd made it! Bud, undoubtedly, was an ace.

Chapter 30
Greetings

I imagined the shock they must've experienced when Bud asked them to bring a wheelchair to the landing site.

Two planes out of three had made it back, two of Rezo's men out of six -- one killed, three imprisoned in Russia. We could only grieve for the perished, but we could probably do much more to save those apprehended in Sochi.

I knew a whole bundle of problems was waiting for my return, but they would bother me later. All I felt was joy and relief. Not being shot at, threatened, or about to die for a few hours – that was something a little forgotten, given the sequence of the latest events.

A two-thirds empty bottle of scotch, an ashtray full of cigarette butts, half a bottle of tonic – all spread around me -- evidenced a spontaneous celebration party I organized for myself, once the danger had subsided. Rezo seemed disapproving, but agreed to clink glasses a couple of times. Adrenaline surging through my body countered the alcohol and didn't let me descend into drunkenness.

A storm front that we needed to pass through on the way to London and the endless circling above the airport until we got the permission to land were nothing in comparison with what had preceded them.

We were still taxiing to the parking when I saw all the people waiting for me: my dear wife with our kids and it seemed our entire London office. Dozens of people. My heart stung when I saw my family. With all the biz and other routine, I had neglected them for a long time. What's important and what's not become especially clear when confronted with life- threatening situations. I hadn't forgotten my resolution, and I would compensate my kids and wife for the absent father situation they had needed to cope with for a long time.

The smiles, the joy, were all sincere. The champagne they eagerly opened. Maybe a softy in recent years, I didn't consider myself a good and easy man and boss to work for, so seeing all of them cheering for my release wasn't something I took for granted. If people cared, I'd care back. I embezzled, cheated, squeezed, extorted and did lots of other stuff, but I didn't let my people down. Ever. Maybe that was what they found in me and offered their loyalty in exchange. I was touched, and the booze fueled the feelings even more.

"Mishenka, let's go to the hospital!" My wife was terrified by my physical shape.

I hugged her, really strong, reigniting the long forgotten or rusted feelings. I had someone to survive for. Her and my kids, who joined the family hug.

There were upbeat voices all around; somebody was pouring champagne again and again. There were some airport officials, dealt with diligently by David and Sasha. They would have my hug too in due time. In fact – now.

Rezo put me into the wheelchair and I asked him to bring me to David and Sasha. They gladly interrupted their discussions with the authorities.

Drunk, elated, detached, this was one of the happiest moments of my life.

***

I couldn't rest on my laurels forever. After a few days I was partially back in business. The orthopedist gave me some hope, promising to fit a top-notch artificial leg so that I "wouldn't feel the difference." Even if I divided his words by two, it was something I was looking forward to.

David meticulously updated me on the latest developments and the "organization" that had supposedly taken me over from Suzy and kept me in custody.

Our "guest" piqued my curiosity enough to invite him for a personal chat.

Since Rezo was the one who had rescued me, he was by my side these days, naturally occupying a function ranging from a bodyguard through custodian to confidante.

I asked him to warm up Paul or Pavel (our guest used both English and Russian versions) for me. According to Kevin's and Rezo's heads-up, he wasn't exactly a hero ready to die without giving away his secrets.

When I opened the door and advanced in with my wheelchair, I saw an angry middle-aged dude handcuffed to the table, a trickle of blood running from his mouth, spitting angrily on my clean floor and an even angrier Rezo shouting at him, "... manners. I'll show you some."

Hearing or feeling me behind his back, Rezo turned around. "All yours, this bastard. He needs to learn some respect."

I put my palm up to silence him and addressed Paul. "Hoped to never see me, didn't you? Why did you crave my life and fortune?" I knew these were big questions for a starter.

The captive conspirer didn't care to deny. "You are an embodiment of evil and one of the tops. We want your stolen funds to finance our programs, and we want your life, so others will fear for theirs, that there is someone after them. Stealing from a thief is blessed." He spat some more blood on the floor.

An insolent cunt. I was studying his reactions.

"So, I'm a proverbial scapegoat? How flattering. About 'stolen money' – you might not know, but roughly two-thirds of my businesses are brand new, meaning I initiated them from scratch and therefore being the first proprietor, I couldn't have stolen them."

"It's all stolen nonetheless through underpaying employees, disrupting competitors, abuse of your connections with the authorities, monopolizing natural resources," he seemed vehemently convinced.

"That's just a bunch of stereotypes, nothing more," I grinned. "On the other hand, some of those stereotypes aren't exactly baseless. Less so in my case, although admittedly I do have a few entries in my business curriculum that I'm not very proud of."

My smile became broader. I liked to express myself ambiguously so that the other person might get confused about what I meant. Sometimes I wasn't sure about the meaning myself, rolling it about my mind as I spoke. Furthermore, I liked those idealistic chaps, confident that they came to save the world. For someone like him, I was indeed a perfect target or a showcase even.

"Tell me, Pavel," I translated his name into Russian. "Say you got some of my money – getting it all would entail a long process of alienation, since most of my fortune is in corporate rights, funds, derivatives, real estate and all. What would you do next?"

"Recruit people; use media resources and social network campaigns to promote our ideas, to open people's eyes on how they are being fucked by someone like you; choose next targets. A lot of stuff. Some of it we are doing with whatever little funding we already have."

"Nice." I was cynical, of course; however, some of it did have appeal. "Looks like you've lots to do. And it's not something undoable even. There are what? Maybe only a couple thousand billionaires at the moment, so getting them all is not like colonizing Mars. Who's your target audience, by the way?"

"Anyone, most of the Western public, disillusioned about stable present and rosy future. Maybe Americans a little less, as their society is of 'winners' and 'losers,' a system praising individual success. They attribute failure to themselves, while the system has lots to do with it too. The American dream could be stolen while no one noticed.

Harder to evoke sympathy and cohesion and get rid of the Communist stigma."

At this stage I only half listened, analyzing. "Maybe I can do something with all this," I murmured to myself, with no intention for Paul to hear.

I pressed 2 on the phone on my desk and Jane, my secretary, stepped in.

"Please, wipe these stains on the floor," I pointed towards the blood splattered around, "and give this gentleman something to clean his face. Do you want anything to drink?" Now I addressed Paul.

"Yes."

"Bring him water, please."

Jane disappeared behind the door.

I used the pause to wrap my head around the situation. Maybe much more than business instincts, I had a flair for recognizing opportunities and turning them to my favor. Some little tinging at the bottom of my head hinted that I was presented with one.

Returning from thoughts to dialogue, I continued. "And what's the endgame? Some sort of lousy Communism, where once again everyone's poor and there is no stimulus to compete and succeed?" Interested in the approach and the actual willingness to change things, I needed clarifications to see whether it could be something handy.

"The endgame? Well, having you parasites dethroned is quite an achievement in itself. Not sure about Communism, but social and economic justice are indeed among our goals. Bridging the gap, saving our countries from poisonous greed." Paul seemed enthused to share his vision, even with the bitter enemy.

"Ha-ha, you should go for crowdfunding with these ideas and see how fundable is social and economic justice and how soon you are tagged as a Commie." I laughed at my own joke.

The idea started to hatch, now shaping into something more actionable. I needed to digest what I had heard, and I also needed a full "X-ray" of the activities of these Marxist clowns.

I thought I'd figured out the big picture. Now I still lacked a few details.

I toughened my voice and became fully focused.

"Who gave you the idea to kidnap me?"

Paul must've thought we'd finished. He now looked up at my face and understood the foreplay was over. There was no trace of a joking mood on my face anymore.

"Err, KGB."

I hoped he had opted to tell the truth. "Why?"

"They mentioned some old scores, but said that there is no sense in targeting number two, three, or five. It's best to go for *numero uno*. The next in line would get the drift. They'd done something similar with the richest man in Russia, I think."

"I see." So far it sounded plausible to me. "Is Suzy your gal or KGB's?"

"Hard to tell. KGB gave me a tip to contact her and told me how to approach and convince her that we shared a common interest, but I'm not sure she works for them. She rather struck me as a loner."

"Who is Vitaliy Aksentyev?" I had memorized the name on the driving license of the guy I had shot when escaping my custody in Russia.

"I don't know him well. He's one of our strongmen. The Russian branch. Ex special forces or something. Our Russian sponsors used to recommend their retirees to staff our military wing both in Russia and in the West."

"Interesting - a paramilitary, hybrid political-militant organization. What a world we live in." I sighed.

"Were you supposed to share the monetary loot with your sponsors?"

"Well, yeah, they ran the finances. Whatever we would have managed to extort was supposed to go to the account they gave me."

Old habits die hard, I thought to myself. Once an enemy – always an enemy for them.

I asked Rezo to take me out, and once out of sight I gave him further instructions. "This organization interests me. Try not to kill this Paul and maybe even switch the tone and treatment, but I need their full organizational chart, their leaders, who exactly contacts him, who's responsible for their finances, what they did up until now, who their members are, geographic coverage, whatever you can procure."

Knowing Rezo's diligence, I could count on getting it with cautious optimism.

"Let Kevin in on this task, too." He had brought him in and deserved to participate in cracking the nut.

Chapter 31
Old "friends"

Suzy called. I knew she would. Probably heard about my miraculous escape, surrounded by mystery and undisclosed details, which the press always distorts and exaggerates. As I insisted, my people declined any comment, then so-called "reliable sources," orchestrated by my spokesman, reported various stories, ranging from me being rescued from cannibal tribes in remote parts of New Guinea to my escape from the CIA's facility in Guantanamo. Some made me smile, some others – frown, but I couldn't possibly rebut them without providing my own version. And that was a price I was unwilling to pay.

Just like in good old times, she arrived to my London office. The woman responsible for killing my friend and security chief as well as for my recent imbroglio with a very near escape. Before she could see me, she had to pass through a diligent and likely rough security check. I didn't interfere. It was for my safety, which I had learned to cherish.

Finally, they brought her in. Red blouse, black miniskirt -- and arms handcuffed behind her back -- didn't match too well. She looked seductive as ever and was fully intent to play this card.

I rolled out from behind the desk in my wheelchair.

"Leave me the keys and leave us alone," I ordered firmly to the guards. If she had come to finish me, she would need to do it with teeth and legs.

"Misha, I was wrong, I apologize." Rarely moved, the wet of her eyes was barely noticeable.

"You know where I come from. In our world apology means nothing. You killed my man and almost got me killed. What's the retribution for this?" Her regret was almost absurd and changed nothing.

"I know I deserve to die. Worse – I killed someone I loved and that's something more painful than you could possibly offer, including death." She meant it, I felt.

"Why are you here?"

"Because I feel I owe you one."

She came closer and somewhat cautiously sat on my lap. Her eyes on the keys meant a silent request to unlock her. Hesitant for only a moment, I reached for them and set her free. Undoubtedly a weakness, I usually took these romantic risks. She wrapped her left arm around my neck – a gesture of lust, not of a threat.

"Yes, you do. Big time. Seducing me is not such a hard feat to change anything." I wanted her. At the time, I had given up on her in Arthur's favor, but now I could hardly resist.

"I know." She started unbuttoning my shirt.

Of course, I was game (*for the last time,* I thought to myself), if anyone cared to ask. I already knew I'd hate myself afterwards for being a reckless youngster again.

Extracting her pair of boobs tantalizing my nose was just a matter of a second. The wheelchair wasn't exactly my favorite for this kind of activity, but I looked forward to a position or two that it availed.

She waited until I kissed her nipples to kiss me on my lips. Somebody knocked or entered and retreated hastily in embarrassment. I didn't care, as the surging libido engulfed us or at least me. I used to like this kind of "negotiation."

***

"You are predictable, Misha." Suzy got off my lap when the abrupt passion came to its logical ending.

"In my love to women?"

"Love? I'd call it sexist objectification." Judging by her tone, Suzy wasn't too serious about this accusation, though.

"That's where you are all wrong. Some maybe think of me as sexist, misogynistic, whatever, but I'm indiscriminate in my use of both men and women to my needs." I laughed, still elated by the encounter.

"That's some dubious glory."

"Don't know about glory. That's my cynical self-evaluation. And you know what? I do it from love, not hatred or disrespect. However, it's not me that needs to defend his acts. To my voluntary credit though, I should say, I mean no harm to men or women alike, unless they try to hurt me, my family, or my near circle. In your case, you did that, and it's not something pardonable."

We may have fucked, but friends we were not. We both knew the score. A tense silence hung in the office.

Betrayal was unforgiveable. Yet, it came from the angle of vengeance for her brother, for whose death she wrongfully held us responsible. I felt like the Godfather, deciding the fate of people. I had an idea about what to do with her; I needed to sleep on it.

She waited for my verdict, maybe prepared to accept anything.

"I'll let you know." I turned around, meaning the "audience" was over, slightly regretful about indulging in my Achilles heel when it came to women. After all, I had told myself I needed to stop it. I meant it and I would.

The explosion outside almost threw me off the chair, while the shockwave shattered all the windows. It meant I had pressing affairs at hand.

Chapter 32
Explosion

It was my armored Bentley. Moving around with a wheelchair, I made it to the scene among the last ones. The car was lying on its roof, splintered into two halves.

I wasn't materialistic and didn't connect to things, although I loved this car, fitted to my exact requirements. Its matte black color symbolized its destruction in these circumstances.

David rushed to me with a piece of paper in his hands.

"Here, taken out from the mail box. Look."

I unfolded it. "You have until midnight to release Paul," it read.

These fuckers wanted war. They'd get one. All my thoughts on how to deal with Suzy fell into place, solving the puzzle in my head. She was still here, standing on the sidewalk at some distance, composed, as far as I could assess. Once again, like in old times, I felt focused and in charge.

"Police, fire department, spooks, everyone will be here. You take care of them, David. Sure, it's an assassination attempt on me. We don't know who's behind it and all the blah, blah. No word about the note, of course." I knew David would handle it even with one hand tied behind his back.

"Of course," David nodded. "We need to talk, though."

"Yes, we do. After all the mess is cleared, invite my brother Kevin and Rezo to our screened room." We'd built this facility some time ago, minimizing the possibility to eavesdrop from afar and near, in which everyone had to leave a switched-off cellphone and put it into a drawer.

"Have Suzy waiting ready to be called inside."

I returned to the building to pour myself something to calm down.

I needed all the details, locations, contacts, specifics, everything about the military wing of these "proletarian fuckers," and I needed them now.

I asked the secretary, who'd been extremely worried but pretended to stay cool, to call Rezo to my office. She tried to hide or suppress it, but I noticed her trembling fingers and bitten lips.

"You know me, Jane, I attract troubles like a magnet. Someday you'll have your sigh of relief at my funeral." They were all used to my cynical humor, the downside of which was that it didn't lift their spirits.

"Give yourself a few more years, we'll withstand it," she smirked, and I was glad that I had managed to raise her morale a little. Employees needed that; otherwise, they couldn't survive working alongside me for a meaningful while.

***

Rezo seemed tense.

"Relax, my friend, we just escaped a much scarier trap, not to perish at the hands of some fuckers." With Rezo I assumed a more sinister guise.

"They are a serious threat. I've scrutinized a series of seemingly unconnected incidents involving accidents, mysterious disappearance of funds, kidnapping among the wealthier part of humanity – all unresolved by the authorities, and I suspect that many of them connect to this proletarian union. At this stage, they already have a global reach, funds, worshipers, backers, and capable executioners."

"Sounds like our league and, with all that, we have their leader tied and bleeding, sitting in our basement. How's that?" A rhetorical question. I didn't underestimate them for a second, yet I wasn't about to buckle my knees in fear.

"We need to make a move," I continued. "Procure or beat out details about their hit force. If we can deal with their militants, I'll find a way to come to terms with their 'political' leadership."

"Yes, in this you are the best, no doubt." Flattering the boss couldn't be wrong. Many of them still had this Soviet mentality.

"I want to use Suzy on this." I didn't need corroboration for my decisions, but nonetheless wanted to hear his opinion.

"For a suicide mission? That would be smart." Rezo thought I wanted to literally kill two birds with one stone.

"Not precisely. I want her to have a fair chance to return alive. That'll be her redemption or retribution, whatever the outcome."

"I see you become a little soft with age." Rezo didn't sound reprimanding, though -- more appreciative.

"Probably." I conceded the obvious.

"Try to have the data today. We are nearing the showdown," I urged him, so he stood up and left to perform.

Chapter 33
Intel first

I didn't want to know, nor did I care about the methods: I expected results, and Rezo delivered.

A neat dossier, although thin, contained all the details of the top three commanders of the military wing of the "union." Two Russians and one Canadian. Rezo swore he had even managed to cross-check the info and found it correct. If we managed to take out the top man and possibly one of the deputies, it'd take them time to recuperate and maybe they'd leave us alone altogether. Fanatics or not, I assumed they still wanted to live. Kamikaze, ready to sacrifice themselves, usually didn't make it to the top.

Suzy patiently sat by my desk waiting for me to pass her the dossier. She kenned the score and anticipated the task and the risk it involved.

The faces in the photos didn't tell me much, but all of them looked military type – with firm chin, prying gaze and bossy bearing. All my business career I had been surrounded by that type, either as bodyguards or adversaries. I finally passed the file to her.

She looked briefly through it, and I thought I captured a glimpse of recognition on her face.

"Whom do you know among them?" I demanded.

"This guy. Number two. Pierre something. A serious fighter and strategist as far as I know." Suzy didn't show much emotion.

Neither did I. I wouldn't mind repeating our little sexual union from the previous day, but I had promised myself not to, and it didn't feel appropriate to the moment.

"Would you have trouble whacking him?" I couldn't believe I was basically ordering a hit.

"None at all." Even if she would, she knew how to play poker face.

"Can you do it alone? You know I need the boss and at least one of the deputies dead, more than I want to put you in danger. Having you killed wouldn't be that disastrous, but that's not the main point." I was frank and direct, knowing that she perfectly understood my deliberations.

"I can do it." Very laconic on her part.

"We don't have much time and you can use any financial or logistical support you may need in planning the operation. I'll ask Rezo to take personal care to this end."

"Thanks. You'll hear from me." She was leaving. "… Or maybe not."

"Good luck."

Chapter 34
Tectonic change

I had been thinking about it for a while. The organization, whose leader we kept against his will, had a point.

Reaching the top of the economic heap the way I had, and the way I knew many others had used, exposed inherent weaknesses in the economic competition. Productive and progressive as it was while competing, it became oppressive and destructive once the winner in a certain area was clearly decided. And this happened in many industries, nowadays more than ever. The "winner" just bought out any threat to his or her (rare) dominance or derailed competitors by hook or by crook, using endless monetary resources for lobbying, bribery, damping, and all other seemingly prohibited methods. Been there, done that.

I dealt with competitors heavy-handedly and so did most of my peers.

Having the world cornered into fewer and fewer hands didn't look right to me, even if one pair of hands was mine. A healthy ecosystem meant a large enough base of customers able to earn decent incomes and spend money on all the shit that was on offer, so that we, the industrialists, could have constant external influx of funds.

Otherwise, it would mean turning to neo-feudalism, where capital and assets are concentrated with the uber-rich, who would need to support the unemployed or starving subordinates to prevent hunger riots.

Yeah, these were dystopian, hungover thoughts that I sometimes shared with David and Sasha and argued with them.

Did I want to revolutionize the system or waive my own fortunes? Now I wasn't that naïve. But I wanted to have a lever on others and maybe on myself, which Paul's organization offered.

Its communist coloring didn't bother me. I wasn't American, although I had my own problem with specific pseudo-Communists responsible for the death of my father and those substituting a free world with suppressive and homogeneous ideology of the former USSR. The idea *per se* had some appeal, and were it not for Communists, I wasn't sure we'd be talking about a fairer world with reasonable working hours, vacations, benefits and other stuff.

Resorting solely to "acceptable" means couldn't be adequate when those in high positions clearly held all political levers through sponsorship and lobbying.

To safeguard the world, as pompous as it sounds, I needed additional instruments. Yeah, I had become a megalomaniac, I knew it, but what else can one turn to when already rich and bored, especially if I was gonna give up on my weakness for the ladies? The change, or at least the balance, wouldn't come from the business level, as no one could objectively evaluate his own act, not talking about self-restraint; nor would it come from a political echelon, engaged in survival, personal agenda, and ass-licking.

I was a practical philosopher, though, if such a thing wasn't an oxymoron, and I designated Paul a big role in my future plans. I tried to transform our relations from prisoner and imprisoned to a more friendly footing. The older me preferred turning enemies into useful instruments over wiping them out.

"Say what, my dear friend Paul, since you were after my funds, what you gonna do if I give them to you?" I teased him, having him seated in front of me without bracelets, sipping on one of the most expensive single malt whiskeys. It wasn't hard to corrupt people.

"You've asked me that already. We'll grow our organizations, try to stand up to fuckers like yourself." He kept to his initial rhetoric but his 'fuckers like yourself' didn't sound that menacing anymore.

The pleasure of tormenting my proletarian guest was rudely interrupted by David, who barged in with his usual, "You gotta see it," placing his cellphone on a coffee table separating Paul and myself.

Paul grasped the news displayed on some internet resource much faster than me. He knew the victim, his face distorting in outrage.

"Political activist found dead in his apartment," read the heading, and the article described "traces of fighting and resistance."

Suzy! The uncensored pictures from within the apartment were already on my cellphone, as I quickly discovered.

Blood and destruction everywhere, accompanied by Suzy's note from undisclosed cell phone "-1."

"Well, you look at mine," I said, extending my cellphone to David. "One of the deputies, supposedly number two, is down."

Paul's pale face told it all.

As it frequently happens in life, a positive streak appeared to be short-lived as these guys were more proactive and agile than we could have imagined.

Chapter 35
Sauna

As I learned *post factum*, the blow was two-fold.

My idiotic security detail had been fooled by a substitute fake plumber, who on his third visit, when they had already gotten used to him and suspected nothing, let more combatants into the building, which he already knew all too well by then. No one was hurt, but Paul was gone, together with a few hard discs with god knows what sensitive info they might contain. All that while I was having a dinner with my three colleagues from Ukraine paying a visit to London.

Sauna, vodka, and girls were-old school celebration, but we were all pre-millennials with die-hard habits.

I liked this place and used it a lot for hosting friends and dignitaries. Renovated in modern high-tech style, it offered a large pool, a spacious sauna with a smaller circular one close to the heat cabin, and a big hall that could be arranged for anything. Usually, and this time too, it contained a table big enough for twenty people, with simple wood benches around it. For the right amount, the owners would readily avail privacy on request, renting out the entire place to me and letting me bring my own personnel to replace theirs.

After enjoying water and heat pleasures, we were well into the meal. Two of the girls that I knew my Ukrainian friends would want for dessert were with us; maybe more waited in the lobby with my bodyguards.

Dmytro had just finished his third toast, "To women!" with a traditional "na zdorovye," when gunshots and ensuing girls' shrieks made me spill my vodka and ruined our happy reunion.

I had left four guards in the lobby, plus Dmytro and Serge had come with two of their own. Yasha hadn't come with any. Six trained dudes against an unknown number of assailants. I did this quick math in my head, while looking hastily for my cellphone to call Rezo or Kevin to send reinforcements. *Where the hell did I put it?*

I was the first to come around after the immediate shock. "Dmytro, lock and block the door. Move this heavy table over there."

I tried to help but couldn't, and stumbled with my artificial leg, attached for the first time only yesterday. The leg needed to be "washed," meaning "drunk to," according to our old tradition, and was one of the main reasons for celebration.

There was no backdoor out of here. I looked up at the windows in hope. We were on the ground floor, which gave us a fair chance to escape, unless of course the adversaries expected us.

The shots died down and somebody was trying to pry the door open. *Shit, they killed the guards* was my prime thought. A white gown and my dick weren't the best gear for armed confrontation.

"Shut the fuck up," I yelled at the girls, as their sobbing was distractive and irritating.

Gun shots at the lock meant we had to do something or surrender.

"Yasha, let's use this chair and try to climb out." I passed one to my old friend. He climbed on it and attempted to open the window placed above his height just below the ceiling. Instead it was shattered, knocking Yasha back, and someone jumped in.

I covered my face to avoid splinters and then I saw him -- no, it was her. "Suzy!" I yelled in surprise.

"Hello. Move back to the pool in the other room. I'll deal with it. The reinforcement is on the way." She was authoritative and business-like, with maybe a slight disapproval on her face at girls and booze, understanding though the purpose of our get-together. "Don't use the window. I killed two assailants. They will send more."

We retreated to the pool, but I couldn't just sit there, so returned just in time to see the door busted with some ram, greeted by Suzy's round of fire from a compact submachine gun, probably an Uzi. The events unfolded like in a videoclip, while I was simply registering them. Somebody shrieked, yelled, gulped. The bullets had connected.

Through the dust I saw an empty corridor. Suzy didn't wait and hurled a grenade into the corridor leading to the spa.

Blow, wave, tremor, dust, more shrieks. Most importantly, she had kept them at bay for a few secs.

Another grenade. *Shit!* They had thrown one in, too. It rolled just in front of my feet.

"Back away!" We retreated and Suzy jumped on me, so we both fell into the pool, followed by the inner doors blown off behind us by the explosion. Shrieks on our side. It was the second hooker, moaning over her dead friend, blood pouring from a cut caused by the debris propelled by the explosion straight into the pool.

Shocked, wet, and desperate, we were cornered inside the pool; however, Suzy didn't intend to surrender, ready to shoot anyone appearing at the corridor opening, still pretty much intact despite the explosions.

A few seconds passed, but no one approached. Then we heard a heavy gunfight getting a bit farther from where we were. *Reinforcements?*

More rounds, shooting coming closer and then dying down. *Who came out with the upper hand?* A panicky thought crept into my mind.

Chapter 36
Rescue

"Don't shoot!" Thank God, it was Rezo's voice!

"It's friends," I told Suzy to avoid friendly fire. We climbed out of the pool in time to greet Rezo, pushing some tied fucker in front of him, with more fighters behind him.

"Oh, man. You saved my ass for the second time! How did you find out?"

"Suzy called. She said she was on the way and that these cunts had laid an ambush for you in the spa."

I eyed Suzy, estimating her not-less-pivotal contribution to our rescue.

"Thanks," I said to her dryly, still unable to let go of all the grudges that had piled up.

She nodded, probably understanding my mixed feelings. Well, she deserved her pardon; I couldn't order her execution after this.

With all the bullets flying around, it was a miracle that the bottle of vodka wasn't shattered. Dmytro, with trembling hands, grabbed it, said "LeHaim" for some reason, took a huge gulp and passed it on to me.

What the heck, I took a big gulp too, awaiting the soothing effect. I recalled reading somewhere that Fidel Castro had survived hundreds of assassination attempts initiated or sponsored by the CIA. With all these violent events, I hoped I wasn't about to beat his record, and I felt I couldn't push my luck any longer.

The leader of the military wing was among the dead bodies scattered around the place. Taking him out early had allowed Rezo to subdue the demoralized fuckers relatively quickly.

The captured dude's involuntary tip-off after application of only mild force enabled us to get Paul back, as we swiftly visited his hide-out in Eastern London.

***

After the recent events, I couldn't stay in London anymore, as the authorities wouldn't let us breathe without heavy supervision. I could understand them; they didn't want all the mess that followed me everywhere.

Money loves quiet. With all the attention, I didn't feel comfy. Besides, Brexit and stuff made London less attractive as my holding's headquarters.

Ukraine, on the other hand, having regained new consolidated leadership and a promising economic future, lured me back. Masha felt the same, although the kids were reluctant to sever ties with their London friends and entourage.

Before leaving, I had business to accomplish. And Paul, now looking not less billionaire than me, with a cigar in one hand and a fine single malt in the other, sitting across from me, was the key figure thereof.

"It's money time, my friend, or if you prefer a more proletarian flavor...," I chuckled, unable to finish the sentence. "What I offer you is a Marx-Engels partnership, where the much richer Engels financed a poor but talented Marx."

"I'm flattered to be compared with Marx; however, Engels would turn in his grave featuring you in his role." Paul was cynical, but he didn't sound as if he opposed the idea.

"Ha-ha, who knows?" I was elated sensing the deal.

"You are hardly a philanthropist, Michael, so giving me some dough, you'd expect a return. What will it be?" He was an idealist – yes, naïve – not very.

"You'd be surprised, but I kinda share your vision, coming from within. Most glorious empires fell and disintegrated because their leaders lacked self-restraint. We all, and I'm talking about filthy rich like myself, are involved in a hard struggle, nourishing our superego to succeed and to best everyone else in the game. It's hard to stop, look around, and spot the devastating effect an ultimate victory has. Once you or I or he is on top, we won't let anyone near it, using any means at our disposal. From something positive it turns disastrous. I need you there to check this sometimes cancerous proliferation."

"The best thing would be a reshuffle of material goods once in half a century maybe, so those who come to the game late, like kids born into this world, won't feel the game is rigged before they even join it." That was one of Paul's ideas for a better society.

"As you understand, it's completely opposite to accruing capital and striving to climb the charts, but I see a lot of logic in what you are suggesting. Nobody needs to starve just because a few dudes managed to put their hands on lands, crops, industries, or whatever even before he or she was born." We were carving out a mutual agenda. "So back to the bottom line – we can coordinate our efforts in improving our societies: you from the outside and I from the inside. One of my nightmare scenarios is that a class struggle and a growing gap will topple order, which then turns into chaos within days. The better and stronger the order, and the more comprehensive it is with regards to all the layers of population, the harder it becomes for subversion."

Paul nodded and sipped on his whiskey.

"A deal?" I raised my glass.

He looked at me, scanning my face for a sign of dishonesty and, after probably satisfying himself, replied, "Ok, deal, cheers!"

We clinked glasses. Everything could change, and our moment of concord could be torn apart, but at this stage I could leave London with a lighter heart.

Maybe I knew how to come to terms with some bitter enemies but, unfortunately, I couldn't revive those fallen in the days of hostilities.

Chapter 37
Returning home

Supposedly, it was a "New Ukraine." So far, "old" and "new" were just the same, as corruption and connections continued to be much more important for success than brilliant ideas, business skill, or talent of any kind. Budgetary funds were borrowed from the West and collected from businesses and population, but largely distributed among those close to the ruling junta and stolen through considerably inflated contracts.

Courts and law enforcement were governed by dough and shady bosses, responsible for their control on behalf of regime's favorites.

The cash country. Where do you think all the printed dollars have disappeared? I had an answer – many of them were here, stashed in Ukraine: under the flooring, in the vaults, bank deposit boxes, caches or impromptu hiding places. The real thing, not some plastic cards or cellphone apps. If you had many, you were a king – little, and you sucked. Most sucked.

Unlike Russia, though, it offered much more freedom, pluralism, and decentralization.

No wonder Ukraine "boasted" two revolutions and instances of severe political turbulence throughout its short history of less than thirty years.

Yet, it was home. Kiev or Kyiv (go figure which is righter) was my city. Living abroad had changed my worldview and mentality, but these were still my people.

Coming out from another uninvited "adventure," I felt fed up with struggles, be they for money or for cause. Maybe I'd softened, but I didn't feel ashamed. Abroad, "soft" didn't necessarily mean "weak"; however, in Ukraine, the attitude might still be different.

Yeah, the word "retirement" had crossed my mind more than once. I knew I couldn't fish, read, or write memoirs to satisfy my usual drive for action, but I could maybe scale it down and find less ambitious goals.

I had never just adopted someone else's opinion, nor had I respected anyone so deeply as to be influenced; however, I loved to bounce my thoughts off people I trusted and liked. For this purpose, Sasha and David were my natural choice, as Boris and Arthur would've been, too, were they still around.

What could be better than a dinner at a restaurant on Dnieper hills overlooking the river and huge neighborhoods crowding its flat left bank from the shore to the horizon?

I picked up David on the way, while Sasha was first to the restaurant, already sampling some pickles and the Ukrainian version of "tapas" - small toasted breads with slices of peppered pork fat on them. Maybe not very healthy, but perfect for a starter and as a backup for a shot of vodka.

This was the same traditional cuisine restaurant where we used to hang out twenty years younger and where we brought regularly our foreign delegations to immerse them in local folklore.

I insisted on no wives, mistresses, or girlfriends for the purpose; therefore, after we ordered and quieted our hunger with appetizers, I proceeded straight to the biz.

"We have a very good reason to celebrate, as all Rezo's people were released from detention in Russia. Cost me a small fortune, but finally they are on the way back to Georgia this very moment. Na Zdorovya!" I raised a shot glass filled with frozen vodka; we clinked and downed one each.

After a few gulps of mors to follow the vodka, I continued. "The reason I thought we could meet alone and have one of those philosophical semi-drunk conversations is because I'm contemplating changing direction."

"Don't tell me you are coming out of the closet," David joked, his reflexes still sharp for a humorous exchange.

"Not quite, but in a sense. My entire life I've been chasing wealth, often sacrificing a lot to win the battles, accumulating more and more. But I've always considered moolah as the means, not the purpose. Now I want to spend it, some of it, most of it, I don't know." That was the punch line of today's get-together, and on this I wanted opinions.

"Oh, Vorotavich the Philanthropist, or Michael the Known Benefactor," David mocked me with Rothschild's nickname.

Friend or not, he just knew exactly how to get on my nerves.

"Cut the bullshit, David, be serious for a sec." I toughened my tone and pretended to be more upset than I really was.

David choked on a pickle, coughed, but didn't give up. "Why? Don't you like it: Michael the Philanthropist?"

"You know what, it does have a nice sound," I consented pacifyingly, "but the main point is not necessarily glory, but rather a new routine, an attempt to change things on global level, a deep tech, of a sort."

Sasha finally joined the conversation, probably contemplating the premise while listening with half an ear to our initial exchange. "Deep tech is indeed the recent fad. A lot of money there," he grinned.

"I never said spending money and making money were mutually exclusive." I retuned a grin of my own. "But still it's not the main point and not a bow in the fad's direction. Maybe I earned my place in Wikipedia for being the richest for a while, but that's not how I want to go down in the history books. Moreover, excelling in moneymaking exposed all the drawbacks of the system. At the end of the day, doing something beneficial can be equally, if not more, satisfactory."

"So, like what?" David assumed a more serious countenance.

"At first - simple things. How about raising salaries to all of our employees by fifty percent?"

"Are you nuts?" David almost jumped out of his chair. "You'll immediately spoil all your figures; consequently, profits will be much lower than predicted and result in a sharp dive on all traded stocks' value."

"Yeah, you are right. But that's a short-lived prognosis. Undoubtedly, there will be a decrease, and some of the value will be wiped out; but, in the long run, it might turn beneficial, as employees will be more committed and simply happier. Read in some paper on the internet about similar precedents. Besides, I believe that if one wants to do something good, it's better to start from those near. They are not transparent; they are our people."

"Oh, Michael the Messiah!" David looked up and positioned his both hands upwards in front of him, as if for a prayer.

It was so comical, I couldn't resist laughing. "Yeah, and David – my right- hand man."

"Thanks, I might pass it up. Not sure I'm built from the required mold." David waved off the idea.

Sasha interjected again to bring us back into a constructive mode. "How do you think your peers will react? It undermines the centuries-long sentiment of paying as little and getting as much as possible."

"True. But I think they'll follow suit. Many of them. In today's world, reputation is extremely important. This looks good on TV, on the Internet, everywhere."

"But what about those who'd oppose it vehemently?" Sasha insisted.

"I hope they won't ken the score until it's too late and it's already a snowball," I reasoned, inventing some of the arguments on the fly. That was exactly why I cherished debates – they availed the medium for arguments and counter-arguments.

I continued, "But that's just a small step, a detail. Raising salaries is nice but it won't bring a change. My vision is broader. Many systems collapsed because the leading echelon lost touch with reality, blinded by their own grandeur. Self-restraint is so anti-individualistic that very few of those who have succeeded and achieved something have it. It's almost mutually exclusive with success. Do you see what I mean?"

"Misha, that's kinda deep. To your title of a Philanthropist, I'm adding the one of Philosopher." David was David.

"Sounds logical," Sasha referred to my thesis. "So, what else were you thinking about?"

"De-concentration, larger redistribution. Groups of interest are skilled to outmaneuver governments and people's interests, but they may have hardships with equal counter-effort, where I can pit my clout, weight, money, and personnel against theirs. And believe me, I'd be able to recruit the best." I was enthusing myself, maybe even more than my brother and best friend.

"And what's the endgame, Mr. Selfless Oligarch?" David wouldn't let it go.

"Don't know, but hopefully – a change felt on the ground. David, maybe you don't remember, since you left for Israel as a kid, but Sasha must. There was a lot of shite in the late former USSR that I happened to mature in, especially anything concerning personal freedoms and wellbeing, but there were no beggars, no one died of hunger; education and healthcare were available to all. It shouldn't be idealized, of course, but I'm certain we can find a better balance between individualism like in the States and Communism like in the USSR."

"Oh, well. You certainly deserve to spend your money as you wish, and I do hope you succeed in bringing the change. If anything, sounds much more attractive than aggressive moneymaking. Count me in, if you need me," Sasha concluded, as two waitresses started to arrange our table with main courses.

Damn, the blond one looks hot, I registered on autopilot, but then cooled myself recalling my undertaken restraint.

Shit. I smiled and maybe David understood my inner struggle.

The food came just in time, as my brother and David needed time to reassess my new vibes. They knew too well that these casual talks would soon transform into action items, as I usually saw my plans carried through.

Cutting accurately the Kiev cutlet to avoid hot oil spattering on my shirt (happened a few times in the past), I saw some movement on David's face. He became rarely serious for a change.

"So, Misha, I've known you what – more than twenty years, right? And I do feel that something different possesses you. The wind of change – remember this song from our youth? The recent events must've contributed, too. I don't feel any more your passion for new deals, projects, acquisitions and all. And your personality needs passion to motivate you."

"I can't claim to have been fully transformed – maybe a little or maybe I'm just oversaturated by moneymaking, but I do have my eyes wide open on a few things. And I do understand my limits and where exactly I'm destructive. I don't want to be. It would be silly if I gave up my pull positions, where I have them, voluntarily, as my competitors will take immediate advantage without giving it a second thought. But maybe I can prepare the ground and do it when we (yes - we) manage to change the game's rules." I paused to have another bite.

"Masha will be happy." Sasha brought the family angle into the equation.

"Yes, she will. It's for her, too. I promised her a few things, except this time – I might hold onto them a little longer." I grinned and they grinned back, as they both knew that I wasn't exactly the most loyal or caring husband. She deserved more from me, and finally I had decided to prioritize it.

Seeing empty plates -- and before full stomachs brought sleepiness and loss of focus -- I returned to business.

"Guys, one of the core things that makes the business world much dirtier than the other life is the belief that we need to play dirty, to do whatever it takes to succeed, that the result is more important than the process. Many of us get up in the morning and "go to war," putting all moral beliefs aside with a phony justification that we do it for our families. You have two different persons: a ruthless cunt while at work and maybe a loving father and a caring friend in the downtime. To change things, we need to cancel this separation between biz and the rest of life, between business ethics and morals."

"That will require a serious mental switch. I know exactly what you mean," David conceded. "And here – no one would want to be the only sucker playing by the new rules. You would also need to change the perception of all those who look at successful businessmen with their mouths open from admiration. They see success and they applaud, while caring less about how it was achieved."

"That's true. Let's have a toast." Sasha poured another round of vodkas, and I took a pickle to be ready with a back-up. "We -- or I should better speak for myself -- I have done a lot of stuff that I'm not particularly proud of. I want to raise this glass that during the time that we have left we'll manage to outbalance our wrongdoings and come to the finish line as the good guys, even if it sounds naïve and idealistic."

Escaping my childhood's poverty or traps laid by adversaries had been difficult, yet escaping my own nature, honed and perfected for moneymaking, could be harder: I hoped not impossible.

We clinked and sealed the deal. And you know what? We've achieved a few things, but that's already a different story . . .

Acknowledgements

Many thanks to Graeme Rodaughan for playing ball and contributing the guest chapter and to Scout from Goodreads/Georgia for her diligent and thoughtful editing and proofreading.

Oligarch Series:

RISE OF AN OLIGARCH, The Way It Is: Book 1, 2014

MORTAL SHOWDOWN, Oligarch series: Book 2, 2015

BE FIRST OR BE DEAD, Oligarch series: Book 3, 2016

ESCAPE?, Oligarch series: Book 4, 2020

www.ingramcontent.com/pod-product-compliance
Lightning Source LLC
Chambersburg PA
CBHW051959220626
47052CB00004B/1015